THE K9 FILES

Dale Mayer

TUCKER: THE K9 FILES, BOOK 13
Beverly Dale Mayer
Valley Publishing Ltd.

Copyright © 2020

ISBN-13: 978-1-773364-37-7
Print Edition

Books in This Series

Boxed Sets and Bundles
https://geni.us/Bundlepage

About This Book

Welcome to the all new K9 Files series reconnecting readers with the unforgettable men from SEALs of Steel in a new series of action packed, page turning romantic suspense that fans have come to expect from USA TODAY Bestselling author Dale Mayer. Pssst... you'll meet other favorite characters from SEALs of Honor and Heroes for Hire too!

Tucker is always ready to fight for the underdog. So when he's offered a mission to save the life of a dog unfairly judged and slated for termination, he can't let her go down without a fight. Plus the dog is in Miami, where his sister lives, and ... no way he can refuse to attend her upcoming wedding.

Addie knows her sister lied about being attacked by the dog, but Addie isn't sure to what extent or how far her sister will go for revenge against an animal she hates. Yet Addie is determined to help the dog who she loves, even if no one else does. Finding a hero to champion her cause isn't part of her plan, but she is quick to realize Tucker's value when she meets him.

Now if only he didn't have a nightmare scenario of his own ... one that threatens to take them all down, including the dog.

Sign up to be notified of all Dale's releases here!
https://geni.us/DaleNews

PROLOGUE

TUCKER WILSON WALKED across the property and stared up at the building, then gave a long whistle. "Man, you guys have worked fast," he said. "The new house had gone up like a dream." He looked over at Badger, who stood there with a clipboard, wearing a hardhat. "I didn't think this was your deal?"

"Until all seven of us have houses," Badger said, "it's *our* deal." He glanced at Tucker, noting the lifelike leg under his shorts, and asked, "How's that prosthetic working for you?"

"Well, it's one of Kat's newest prototypes," he said, stretching it out and twisting the ankle. "A waterproof model while on, apparently. I haven't had a chance to try out that part. And, of course, I've got titanium knees and titanium hip joints now," he said. "I'm almost a rebuilt bionic man," he said with a laugh.

"Join the rest of us," Badger said.

"I've got a hankering for heading home though," Tucker said, looking at Badger sideways. "I didn't say anything about it because I didn't want to slow down your progress, and you've been such a great help getting me back on my feet."

"That's what we're here for," he said, "and, if it's time to go home, then it's time to go home. Nobody can tell you when and where, except for yourself."

1

"Yeah," he said, "it's just one of those things I need to do."

"Any particular reason?"

"My baby sister, Molly, is getting married," he said. "There's just the two of us. She's marrying my old buddy Rodney."

"That's a good reason to go home then," he said. "You thought about work?"

"Well, Rodney's got a construction company, and he wants me to be a foreman."

"Well, you'd do that quite nicely, wouldn't you?"

"Maybe," he said, "but personally I want five acres out in the middle of nowhere and an opportunity to just, … I don't know, maybe raise a few dogs."

"Dogs," Badger said. "You're a dog person?"

He looked at Badger and frowned. "Isn't everybody?"

"Oh no, not everybody is."

"You seem to be running a ton of dog operations through this place. I don't quite understand what that's all about."

"No," he said, "and it isn't always all that clear. But the bottom line is, we're doing a bunch of pro bono work for the War Dog Division."

"I heard about that. You're done though, aren't you?"

"No, they dropped a bunch more files on us. We did the original twelve, and I guess our success has led them to give us a few troublesome cases."

"Great," he said. "Troublesome how?"

"I've got a couple dogs that need rescuing, depending on what quarter of the world you'll be in?" he asked.

"Florida," he said.

"Well, I've got one in Florida, held in a pound, about to

be put to sleep in Miami."

"What? A War Dog?"

"Yes, apparently it attacked a woman."

"And is that confirmed?"

"No. I'm pretty sure nobody gives a shit, and it's just another dog to them," he said sadly. "I've been fighting with them for days."

"Have you got anybody out there to fight on the dog's behalf?"

"No. I'm trying to get them to do DNA testing on the bites, but apparently the woman's refusing."

"Well, that's suspicious as hell."

"She doesn't like dogs," Badger said with a sigh. "So she's not being cooperative."

"Well, Miami isn't exactly my choice," he said. "I don't do huge cities like that. I'm actually from Saint Pete's Beach originally, but, I mean, that's a tourist town. Since my sister's getting married nearby in Tampa though, I'm heading in that direction."

"So no other family?"

He shook his head. "I'm not sure where I'll end up settling. My sister and her soon-to-be husband and his company are based farther out, in a smaller town, where he's doing a couple hundred-unit condo developments."

"So potentially a place where a dog might have a better life?"

"If I have any say about it, yes. Is this one male, female?"

"Female and they're not exactly sure why she turned on and bit her caregiver."

"Aggravation or protecting someone or something," he said immediately.

"Well, that's typical animal behavior. We just don't really know what happened in this case. Nobody's talking. Nobody has any video, and nobody gives a shit. That's the bottom line."

"Yeah, but those dogs have given their lives to the military. The least they deserve is a chance at a decent life."

"She was adopted by the family, and then apparently the parents went on a cruise, and they left her with a daughter, who was attacked."

"And how long was the daughter with the dog?"

"Just a couple weeks."

"*Hmm*," he said. "Well, I can be there first thing tomorrow."

"That would be good," he said, "because I think she's slated to be put down on Friday."

"Two days, counting tomorrow? The dog will die on the same Friday as my sister's rehearsal dinner? That's cutting it really close. Not a whole lot of time."

"Well, I won't be at all upset if you somehow sneak that dog out of lockdown where she is," he said. "We have a little bit of money to help buy her way out, if need be."

"I'll book my flight and head down there right now," he said. "You'll make my sister's day."

"Maybe," he said, "but why don't we make the dog's day and not put her to sleep?"

"What's her name?"

"She's got a big long Latin name, but basically she's Bernadette, and they've shortened it to Bernie."

"That's not a nice name for a beautiful dog," he said.

"She's big, heavily muscled. She's a Malinois with a bit of shepherd thrown in there, typical army breed," he said. "Very well trained and she was a fire dog."

"Well, she should be sniffing out fires then," he said

with a frown.

"Wouldn't that be nice," Badger said. "There, you were looking for a dog, … for a job. Why not that one?"

"It's not exactly construction work."

"Maybe not," he said, "but you have something to do in the interim, if you wanna look for something else."

"Not a bad idea." Just then his phone rang, and he frowned, as he stared down at it. "An SMS message," he said staring at it. "Apparently my soon-to-be brother-in-law has a firebug at one of his condo complexes."

Badger looked at him in delight.

Tucker raised an eyebrow. "You shouldn't look quite so happy about that."

"Maybe not," he said, "but the dog would be perfect to assist on that problem, and we might get a stay on the kill order because of it."

Then Tucker realized what Badger meant. "You got a point there," he said. "I'm on my way. See if you can get us a stay order on the euthanasia."

"Confirm or deny the facts as we know them ASAP," Badger said, "and let me know when you arrive."

"I'll be on the next flight out," he said. "So it all depends on the flight time." He lifted his hand and said, "Nice job for me, by the way."

"If you say so," Badger said. "We're just grateful to have somebody on the animal's side."

"I'm always on the animal's side," Tucker said. "The real predators in the world are the two-legged ones," he said. "The four-legged ones? Well, their behaviors are simple. It's the humans in the world you must watch out for."

And, with that, he turned and walked out.

CHAPTER 1

TUCKER EXITED THE Miami airport the next morning, breathing the heavy air inside. "Certainly not my favorite place," he murmured. Still, it was a far cry from where he had been and where he would have chosen to be, if he had a say. But he was here for a job and his sister Molly's wedding, and that's what counted. At that thought, he heard a honk, and he looked out to see a white new model SUV, pulling toward him, and his sister waving frantically from the inside of the car. He smiled, raced to the passenger side door, and hopped in. "Wow," he said, "that was good timing."

"Of course it was," she said. "I've been tracking your flight the whole way."

"I could have just gotten a rental car here and driven straight to my hotel. A little happy to see me or something?"

"Or something," she said with an impudent grin. "Plus I happened to be down here picking up my wedding dress. As it is, I'm cutting it close, with the wedding in just two days."

"You couldn't find a wedding dress you liked near you?"

"The designer's a friend of mine," she said. "So I came down here to have her do it. And it just so happened to be that you were flying into Miami, so I arranged to pick you up at the same time."

"So you're not staying in Miami?"

"I'll head back to St. Pete's Beach this afternoon," she

said, "and then I'll see you there tomorrow."

"Yeah, I've got to get a rental vehicle. I would have gotten that at the airport, but you stopped that."

"We have a company truck for you, if you want to use that locally," she said. "You're okay to drive?"

"Yes. I've told you that many times. I'm fine to drive. I've been driving for a lot longer than you have."

"Sure, but then I didn't lose body parts and go through multiple surgeries," she said. "I don't know what you're like now."

"I'm fine," he said with a smile.

She gave him a searching glance and then returned her attention to the traffic. "How have you been?"

"I'm fine," he said with that same neutral tone he always used.

She nodded. "Of course you are," she said. "You'd never tell me if you were anything other than that, would you?"

"Because nothing's changed," he said. "What's the point of belaboring the fact?"

"You look better," she said abruptly.

"You didn't see me before," he said with a half laugh.

"Other than initially in the hospital, no, but you're better than I thought, than I expected," she said. "You've got good color in your face. Your eyes are bright. You're standing tall."

"And all those things matter," he said with a nod. "Still hasn't been an easy journey, but I'm here."

"And that's what counts," she said. "We thought we'd lost you there for a while. Of course it didn't help that you wouldn't let any of us come see you."

"You all came and crowded me right after surgery," he said. "I didn't want to see anybody at that point in time, thanks."

"Yep. I know. Rodney and I probably came on a little too strong, didn't we?"

"You think?"

"Hey, it is what it is."

"Did you have to bring Rodney's mom and sister too?" he asked in a mocking tone.

"They were coming with us anyway," she said. "So we just thought that everybody could go to the hospital."

"I can't believe they even let you in."

"We lied," she said cheerfully.

He groaned. "Well, it didn't help my healing in any way."

"And that's why we left," she said, "and it was very hard for me to do. I hope you appreciate the fact that I was looking out for you."

"Of course," he said gently. With just the two of them, it was not hard to see that that had been her motivation. He had just wanted them all to go away and let him sink back under the cloud of drugs. "And it wasn't an easy recovery," he said. "We did stay in touch, but I didn't really want any visitors."

"And I never really understood that, but, any time you got sick, you always wanted everybody to go away. You were like an animal, holed up to either live or die, and you wouldn't come back out again until one or the other had happened," she said, shaking her head. "When I get sick, I want to be held and cuddled. I want somebody to look after me."

"That's why we're so different," he said with a smile. "You've always been like that, and I've always been like I am."

"I know," she said, "but, for somebody like me to be around somebody like you and to not be able to help, it's really frustrating."

"Which is also why you weren't supposed to come," he said, "because you knew I wouldn't want you there, more so because I just wanted to focus on my healing and either *live or die*, as you so eloquently put it," he said with a note of humor. "Or I would be unconscious. Regardless, I didn't want you there while I was trying to get back on my feet. It was a journey I had to take alone."

"But you see? I don't agree with that," she said. "You didn't have to be alone at any time."

He laughed. "Having to be alone is a very different thing," he said, "than choosing to be alone. That's another thing entirely."

"Right," she grumbled. "And, for you, it's always choosing to be alone." She shook her head. "You know that's not normal, right?"

He smiled. "It's normal for me. It's even got a name. *Introvert.*" It was an old argument that they had had—but not recently. "Anyway, once I was back on my feet and was capable of letting you guys know I was doing okay, I did contact you. We've been in touch ever since."

"Yes, but you were alone when you needed somebody," she said, frowning.

"No," he said, "I was alone at a time when I needed to be alone."

"It's very strange," she muttered.

"Only strange for you," he said, "because you're very different from me. But it's the differences that make us work so well together."

She snorted at that. "Basically you just want to be left

alone to do your own thing," she said. "You're not a team player."

"I'm very much a team player," he said. "Yes, it took me a long time to get there, but once I realized that that was necessary for the kind of work I was doing," he said, "I was definitely a team player. But, when you're injured, there's no part of … there's no team in 'I'm injured,'" he said. "It really doesn't matter how much of a team player you are because your team becomes the medical team. And you have to trust that they know what they're doing, or you have to argue your way out of whatever it is that they're trying to talk you into," he said. "At that point in time, there's not a whole lot anybody can do. You have to make your own decisions and follow through."

"But you don't have to be a hard-ass," she said in exasperation. "Other people can be there to help you make those decisions."

"Maybe in your case, yes," he said, "but I'm the one who has to live with the outcome. I'm the one who has to live with the process, the recovery, and whatever I'll have at the end of the day."

She nodded, looking at his leg.

"Missing one lower leg, but new titanium knees and hips," he said cheerfully. "Missing a whole mass of muscle on the one calf, and my back is definitely not pretty, but then I'm not pretty anymore either."

"And never did *pretty* matter to you before," she said. Once again she shot him a long look. He pointed at the highway and said, "Keep your attention on the road. You'll have lots of time to stare at my scars later."

She shook her head. "See? You were always like that," she said. "Even if there weren't any scars, you'd say that."

"Well, the scars are there," he said. "No doubt about it. I'm no poster boy."

"You are, though," she said. "You're a poster boy for courage and bravery."

"I don't think anybody gives a shit," he said. "The world's very much about *me, me, me.*"

"I'm sorry you see it that way," she said. "Because we haven't been through your experiences, it doesn't seem the same for us."

"I wonder," he said. "Your soon-to-be husband might have a different take on that."

"He might," she admitted. "I'm glad you came for the wedding," she said impulsively.

"Well, I'm combining it with another trip too," he said. She raised her eyebrows. He shrugged. "What can I say? I'm here to also help a War Dog," he said.

"But we'll still see you in Saint Pete's Beach tomorrow?" she asked. When he nodded, she added, "I'm just so glad that you survived all of it and that you're here," she said.

"Well, I wouldn't miss my only sister's wedding, particularly when she has no other family."

"And I appreciate that," Molly said mistily. "And you're still okay to walk me down the aisle?"

"That too," he said, wincing ever-so-slightly.

"You don't have a suit, do you?"

He looked at her and frowned. "I thought I could rent one today."

She snorted. "On such short notice? I'm not sure that you can," she said, "and I highly doubt any suit you rent will look any good."

"I'm not that hard to fit. I still take a standard forty-two long off the shelf," he said.

She hesitated and then shrugged. "As long as you show up on time," she said, "I'm fine with whatever."

"Meaning, I could show up in Hawaiian shorts and a big T-shirt?"

"Please don't," she said with a wince.

He laughed. "Okay, I'll try not to."

She gave him a weepy smile. "It's really good to see you."

"Hey, stop the maudlin theatrics," he teased, "and I appreciate the ride."

"I wanted to spend more time here with you," she said, "but just so much has to be done right now."

"You're getting married in two days," he said. "You know that you're expected to be rushed off your feet, but you're supposed to have a lot of help for it."

"I have help," she said dismissively, "but I wouldn't let anybody else pick up my brother."

He smiled at her. "And, once again, I appreciate the ride." They pulled into the hotel he had booked.

She looked at him and said, "You know you could stay with us in Saint Pete's."

"I could," he said cheerfully, "but I can't deal with the dog here in Miami that way."

"I don't understand the dog part," she said, "but I'm grateful that you're here. I was afraid you would find an excuse not to come."

He winced at that because, of course, he had been half planning that. Only as the dog came to the forefront did he decide to grab the late flight to Florida. He'd been waffling over it the whole time. He hated to let her down, but he didn't like crowds and particularly not weddings. As he grabbed his bag that he had kept on his lap, she looked at it and frowned. He said, "It's fine. I'll go shopping, and I'll rent a suit this afternoon."

She looked at him, grinned, and said, "Everything at the last minute, huh?"

He shrugged. "It's not like I've needed a suit for the last few years."

Her smile fell away. "And it wouldn't fit anyway, would it?"

"Nope, sure wouldn't," he said. "I'll rent a vehicle, rent a suit, and I'll be at St. Pete's Beach tomorrow afternoon in time for the rehearsal and afterward the dinner."

With that, he hopped out, lifted his hand to wave, and walked into the hotel. He registered and then asked about a rental vehicle. Thankfully the hotel had arrangements with one of the big local companies, and he quickly arranged for a small truck. If he freed the dog, he needed a way to carry it. The hotel itself wouldn't let him take the dog inside. That was a concern. But he could do some legwork throughout today—both wedding-related and dog-related—stay here tonight and then hopefully figure out what to do after that to rescue the dog tomorrow. He walked up to his room, dropped his bag, quickly searched on his phone for a suit rental, realizing that his procrastination had caused him some last-minute issues.

When he couldn't find anything via a quick internet search, he headed back to the reception desk and asked someone there. The guy quickly sent Tucker down two blocks. As he walked into the store, everybody was friendly and happy, until he said he needed a suit in two days. At that, they stopped and looked at him in horror. He shrugged and said, "If you can't help me, I'll find somebody who can." He added, "I don't need anything but a black suit."

Apparently asking for that was akin to asking for a full-on tux. But thankfully that wasn't the requirement for this wedding. His sister, although she wanted a nice wedding, hadn't required all the stops being pulled out for it.

By then the manager came out and said, "Let's see if we have something in stock for you."

Sure enough, they did. And what could have been a horribly painful and difficult exercise was settled within an hour. They arranged to send the suit to his hotel, which was also good because then he didn't have to pick it up and bring it back. With that taken care of, he carried on back to the hotel, where he asked for directions to a pet store and the pound holding the dog. With directions programed into his phone, he headed out to the rental car area, picked up his truck, and drove to the pet store, just for food and treats. He didn't take long, as he wanted to get to the pound as soon as possible.

It had a large parking lot and was one of those depressing cement buildings. He stared and frowned. "Talk about a lousy place for a War Dog to end up."

He walked inside and approached the woman at the front desk. She looked up at him with a frown. He smiled nicely and said that he was inquiring after the War Dog.

"Ah," she said, "you mean, that shepherd cross."

"Yeah, that shepherd cross, who's won several awards for her bravery in defending our heroes and saving military lives," he said quietly.

She flushed ever-so-slightly.

He realized he was taking his ire out on the wrong person. "Where is she?"

"She's in the back," she said, but she hesitated.

"I'd like to see her," he said firmly.

Again she hesitated.

"Are you telling me that she's not allowed to have visitors? Even prisoners on death row are allowed visitors."

"I just know that this case is being put to sleep," she said.

"Which is exactly why she should be allowed visitors and exactly why we are working hard to get a stay order on her being killed."

"That just extends our expenses to keep her alive," she muttered.

"Meaning?"

"The bill to release her will be high."

He stared at her. "Are you telling me that a dog who risked her life and saved several soldiers many times over isn't entitled to a fair deal?"

She didn't know what to say to that. She got up and hurried into the back office. She returned, following a big strapping male with a huge beer gut on him. He looped his thumbs on his belt loops and said, "What do you want with the dog?"

"First I must positively identify that she's who we think she is," he said, "and then I'll pull a DNA swab from her and get it matched to the bite," he said.

"The victim already has refused that," he said.

"Good, I'm glad to hear that," he said. "We'll see what she says to me when I talk to her."

Immediately the man frowned. "I can't have you harassing her."

"I'm sorry. Did you imply that I would harass somebody?" he asked sharply. "Did I, at any point, say that this woman would deal with something like that?"

"Hey, now, let's just get along here," he said. "We're just following orders here."

"Good," he said. "Then you'll follow US Navy Commander Cross's order right now, which will allow me to see the dog and to confirm identity," he said.

"Do you have something in writing?"

"Do I need it?" he asked in astonishment. "Are you seriously telling me that I can't get in there and confirm who she is? Abuse of animals is a federal crime. Are you not aware of this?"

He just looked from him to the receptionist and back again, and then the manager shrugged. "I guess there's no problem in letting him see her."

"Thank you," he said with exaggerated politeness. He followed the man through a double door to the back of a long hallway, where cages were stacked upon each other. Just seeing the animals caged like this made his heart hurt. He knew most of them would be put to sleep within the week. He just couldn't imagine how a country that was so great and so huge and so wealthy hadn't found a way to solve the lost and abandoned animal problem without trying to kill every single one of them.

As he stepped down the hallway to the second-to-last cage, he saw a large Malinois-shepherd cross curled into the corner, but her eyes were bright and glistening, and her ears were up. She watched every movement the manager made. She stopped, looked at Tucker for a brief second, and then dismissed him, before narrowing her gaze back on the gatekeeper.

Tucker almost felt insulted by that and then realized that she didn't consider him a threat, whereas the gatekeeper was a known threat. "So how badly have you treated her?" he asked quietly.

The manager flushed with anger. "I haven't treated her

badly at all," he said. "Why would you even say that?"

"Because of the way she's watching you. She knows you as a threat, somebody who's already caused her a lot of pain." Tucker texted Badger. **Need K9 military trainer ASAP here at the pound. Got anybody local?** "You will see my navy rep soon on this matter. No more mistreatment of animals will be allowed here by you. And I'll alert the other animal shelters, your local government, including the mayor and the governor." Tucker tilted his head. "Naming you specifically."

He flushed again. "She wasn't cooperative," he blustered. "We had trouble getting her in the cage."

"And you wonder why?" Tucker said, shaking his head. "I need to find out how she ended up at this woman's house in the first place."

"The family adopted her, but they didn't have any idea that she would be a danger to the daughter."

"I want to see your file and the daughter's statement."

The beer-belly guy looked shock. "She told me. Verbally."

"Are you a profit or nonprofit organization here?"

The manager's eyes went wide.

"Do you have no idea about the records you are required by law to keep in relation to each and every animal that comes through this shelter?"

"Well, uh, ..."

"Obviously not. I'll be reporting you on that issue as well."

He stammered about and then finally found his voice. "But her parents took off and left the dog with the daughter."

Tucker stared at the sad excuse of a human being and said, "There are strict rules and restrictions for adopting War

Dogs."

"You take that up with them," he said. "They left the dog with the daughter, but the daughter couldn't handle her."

"There's no *handling* required of a well-trained War Dog, other than food, water, shelter, and love," he said. "Unless the daughter did something to hurt the dog. In which case it doesn't matter if it's a War Dog or any dog, dogs under attack will defend themselves."

"Anyway," the gatekeeper took a step back and said, "there she is."

"I'd like to inspect her, please."

"What good will that do?"

"She's microchipped," he said, once again with that same exaggerated patience in his voice, "as anybody with any knowledge of most dogs would be aware of." In the meantime, he saw the look in the dog's eyes, one of broken trust and fear. "It's okay, girl. The bad man won't hurt you again." Tucker glared at the abuser.

The manager hesitated. "Well, it's your neck," he said. "If she bites you, it just gives me a better reason for putting her down."

With the cage open, Tucker waited for the manager to step back. Tucker stepped inside the cage and closed it and then stood and waited for the manager to leave.

The manager hesitated, and then he shrugged and said, "Hell, if she rips you apart, makes it even easier too."

"She won't," he said with complete confidence, "because I don't abuse animals." Then he turned to sit down at the corner opposite Bernie and said, "Hello, girl. It's been a pretty tough ride these last few months, hasn't it?"

ADDIE ROTTENHEIM WALKED into the living room and looked at her sister, Bernie. "What's the matter now?" Addie asked in exasperation. Her sister lifted a languid hand and brushed back a few tendrils of hair from her forehead. "I've got a headache," she said.

"You've got a headache from the mess you caused," Addie snapped. "What were you thinking?"

"I didn't do anything," she said. "That dog's a menace."

"That dog never hurt a fly," she said. "I'm not even sure how the hell you got her to bite you. You must have been intentionally cruel to Bernie. This has got to stop."

"I hate that dog," she said. "Better that it's long gone. I wish they'd already killed it."

"And I never understood that about you," she said, staring at her younger sister with loathing. "Why would you hurt an animal like that?"

"I'm not hurting it," she said waspishly. "She needs to be put down."

"And why is that?"

"Because she's a danger, and I proved it," she said with a smirk.

"So this all goes back to Mom and Dad getting it for you, and then you not wanting it, huh?"

"They didn't get it for me," she protested, pouting.

Addie shook her head. "You're the one who convinced them that they should adopt this K9 dog because it had the same name as you. What did you think it would do? Come with a handsome soldier at the same time?" she said, staring at her sister. She never really understood what made her sister tick, and it seemed as soon as she did understand one little bit, something changed. "Or was that just because, at the time, you had a military boyfriend, and you thought he'd be impressed that you had a War Dog?"

Her sister glared at her. "It has nothing to do with Ivan."

Addie rolled her eyes. "*Right.* Of course it doesn't. It has everything to do with *you.* Always about you."

Bernie huffed in dismissal. "Besides, Mom and Dad wanted a dog. Remember?"

"Sure they did, but they were looking for a chihuahua. And somehow you managed to convince them, like you always manage to convince them, to get something that you thought they should have. It's called *manipulation.* That's something else that you need to stop doing. To your own parents. To me."

"So what?" she said. "And now we know that that dog was a big mistake. It's not my fault. They made their own decision," she said with a sneer. "Everybody likes to blame me for everything," she said, "but they're the ones who made the decision."

"And they also make those decisions sometimes under pressure, under duress," she said, glaring at her sister. "Bernie, you need help. Professional help."

Again Bernie just ignored that which she didn't want to hear.

Addie knew most of her tricks. Here, as usual, she changed tactics. It's called *diversion.* Addie knew all the terms.

"Well, it's dangerous. They should have shot it weeks ago."

And, for that, Addie almost hated her sister. Bernie was a beautiful dog. She stared at her sister and said, "I want to see the bite. I can clean it for you. I am a nurse, you know? Plus we need to watch out for red striations up and down your leg, which are markers for infection. But don't worry. I bet it's not even bad."

"It is so," she said. "Besides, it doesn't matter how bad it is. The animal's dangerous."

"Not if you're the one who brought about the attack."

"I didn't bring about any attack," she said. "You're always determined to think the worst of me."

"It's not hard." She shook her head, headed out to the kitchen where her purse was. "I'm leaving," she said.

"Wait, wait," she said. "I don't have anything for my headache."

"I guess you'll have to get up and get it then, won't you?" she said callously. And she stormed off, out the front door. She'd come over because their sister had been whining about being in extreme pain, and it hadn't taken very long to realize that her sister was up to her usual games and just wanted somebody to coddle her. It was not a game that Addie played well. But then, with their parents gone on another trip, not too many people were available for Bernie to play her usual games with.

At her car door, Addie stopped for a moment, taking several long deep breaths of fresh air. Her whole family struggled with Bernie. Something was definitely mentally wrong about her. She'd somehow ended up being the most selfish person Addie had ever met.

At twenty-six, Bernie was so spoiled their parents didn't know how to deal with her. It's the reason they took all these long trips. To get away. They hated coming back, and, when they did, they immediately started planning the next one. Bernie had shown no sign of leaving the nest, so their parents left to get away from her. It was a terrible situation, and

Addie had argued with Mom and Dad several times about it, but they were helpless because ultimately they still loved Bernie, even if she was the kind of person you didn't like and didn't want to have around.

Most of the time Bernie was fine; she just needed a lot of extra care and was extremely high maintenance. Mom and Dad had hoped that Bernie would find a boyfriend who'd marry her, but she seemed to burn through them pretty fast.

Addie herself thought that the boyfriends only took so long to figure out just how high maintenance Bernie was before they took a walk. And they never came back. Addie couldn't blame any of them, but, at the same time, she knew her sister did have good points—some ... okay, a few—but it was damn hard to see them sometimes, like right now.

Addie was still so damn angry about the dog. She had yet to even see the bite and had no idea what her sister had done to deserve it, but Addie knew her sister had done something to provoke the dog. So far, all Addie's efforts to save the dog had failed because her sister refused to do anything other than order that it be put down. Bernie had clearly lied and had said that the dog bit her several times. Then changed it to one bite but kept it bandaged. Addie just didn't know why her sister hated the dog so much.

Except for the fact that her sister didn't like anybody who didn't like her, and there was no doubt that the dog didn't like her sister.

To that end, Addie had argued against her parents leaving the dog with her sister because obviously it was a situation that would not go well. But her parents' need to get away from her sister had driven away any concern about whether the dog would be in danger or whether her sister would be in danger. Her sister, was not in danger, but her sister had become a danger to the dog. Addie took another long slow deep breath and opened her car door, as one of the neighbors called out.

"How's your sister doing?" she asked.

"She's doing fine," she said. "Why?"

"Oh, well, she had that terrible dog bite. I'm so glad that dog's being put down."

"Well, the dog didn't bite her," she said. "Bernie just made it up."

The neighbor looked at her, shocked.

Addie shook her head, hopped into the driver's side, and pulled out. She didn't even know what the matter was with her. Well, yes, she did. The dog needed Addie to step up. She had bonded with the dog. Her sister had not. It was what it was. Addie had given up trying to defend her sister a long time ago. It burned her constantly to think that that dog was being put down because of her sister's temper tantrum, her selfish wants. It was a good dog. It was a War Dog, and why the hell did nobody care? Somebody out there must care.

On that note, she headed back to the pound, where she spent so much of her time, trying to find ways to save the animal. She'd even contemplated breaking it out, wondering if she knew anybody who could help her. But figured that, as soon as she did that, her sister would blame her too. And, of course, Addie wasn't the liar her sister was, and would probably 'fess up almost immediately, if somebody asked her if she had stolen the dog from the pound.

She'd also have to find a place to keep the dog, since her place was small, and the Malinois was huge. She had zero fear of Bernie—the dog. But Bernie, her sister? Addie shook her head. She figured that her sister's actions had caused this whole scenario.

Didn't matter how much one loved the dog, it was *still a dog*, it was *still an animal*, and so many had no respect for her as such. Her sister wasn't a dog lover; she was only interested in getting love for herself, and nothing else mattered. To think that the dog and her sister shared the same name just blew Addie away. But it's also how the poor dog had ended up here.

Addie blamed her parents for that too because they weren't prepared to spend the time to help the dog adapt. They thought that her sister, would look after it, and that would free up the parents to leave for all their trips. What a joke. As Addie pulled into the pound, she saw several other vehicles here. She hopped out and walked into the front area.

The receptionist looked up at her, shook her head, and asked, "Still no good news?"

"Of course not," she said. "Can I see her?"

She hesitated and then nodded. "Somebody else is in there too," she said.

At that, Addie stared at her. "Are they putting her down now? You said that she still had a couple days."

"Somebody else is here looking to positively ID her as one of the War Dogs," she said in a low voice. "The boss isn't very happy about it."

At that, Addie's eyebrows lifted because anything the boss wasn't happy about was good news as far as Addie was concerned. She motioned at the door. "Buzz me through, will ya?" Addie had gotten to know the receptionist, Wendy, fairly well this last week or two.

Wendy asked, "How's your sister doing?"

"I don't even think she got bit," she said with a wave of her hand.

"Well, there had to be a doctor's report."

Addie nodded. "Supposedly. I know," she said, "but she sure as hell won't show me the wound."

"Weird," she said.

At that, Addie didn't even bother answering. Her mind was too busy trying to figure out how her sister had gotten a doctor's report written. Addie didn't even know if her sister had a regular doctor who she saw. Maybe Bernie went to an ER somewhere. That nagged away at Addie because none of it made any sense to her.

As she walked to the back all alone, she approached the cage to see a man sitting in the far corner with Bernie herself stretched all the way out, so that her paw rested in the man's hand. She stopped in surprise. "Hello," she said gently.

The man slowly turned to look at her. He smiled and said, "Hello."

She said, "I don't think I've ever seen Bernie here quite so happy."

"Bernie and I've been getting to know each other," he said quietly.

She nodded and said, "This was my family's dog." At that, his smile fell away, and she understood. "It was my sister who got bit," she said in apology.

"Ah," he said. "How badly hurt is she?"

She hesitated, that old loyalty raising its head. "She's not badly hurt," she said with a shrug.

"Which is unusual then that the dog is being put down for something that isn't very bad," he said. "Normally you get several strikes before you get to that stage, and it has to be a bad bite or attack."

"I know," she said. "Apparently, and I wasn't there at the time, my sister said she'd bitten her several times but refused to let anybody know."

"And why is that?"

"I don't know. She says it's too painful to touch the bandage."

"What's your sister's name?"

She hesitated and then said, "Bernie."

He looked at her and looked at the dog, and she nodded. "Yeah, they have the same name. And that's how she convinced my parents to get her the dog."

"Well, dogs like this War Dog, they're still working animals. She was eased into retirement, but she still wouldn't have bitten anybody."

"Well, it's still an animal," she said, feeling slightly defensive.

"Absolutely," he said, "and, as such, she deserves respect and a second chance."

"Well, you won't get an argument out of me," she said. She crouched in front of the gate, only to realize it wasn't locked. She pushed it open slightly and asked, "Can I come in?"

"Do you know her well?"

"I've come many times," she said. "The dog was given to my sister essentially, but Bernie and I have a strong bond. I really miss her."

As she stepped in, Bernie's tail wagged madly. Addie smiled, crouched in front of her, and said, "Hey, girl."

And Bernie immediately bounced to her feet and gave her a huge welcome.

"That's good to see," he said. "I was worried after all the reports I'd heard that she had bitten somebody."

"I'm not worried about getting bit," she said. "It's the euthanasia that's supposed to happen on Friday that worries me."

"I know," he admitted. "I was hoping to find a way to stop it."

"You and me both," she said. The dog licked her face and then calmed down slightly, and Addie looked at the man. I didn't introduce myself," she said. "I'm Addie."

He reached out a hand and shook hers. "And I'm Tucker," he said. "I came on behalf of the War Dog Division to see what's going on here."

She brightened. "Oh, I'm really glad to hear that," she cried out. "Can you rescue her?"

"Well, that's what we're trying to figure out. It seems the dog is being railroaded, and nobody appears to care that she's a War Dog. At the moment it's likely she'll be put down before I have a chance to make a case for her."

"That's something I was trying to avoid." She frowned. "And I don't know what kind of pull my sister had to make this all happen, but I hate it," she murmured, burrowing her face in Bernie's ruff. "Because this dog deserves better."

"But when we're up against the court cases, it's a hard thing to do," he murmured. "They get on this pathway, and to get a stay of an order is much harder."

"And yet this dog didn't deserve any of it," she said.

"Sometimes they do. Sometimes they don't, but I'm glad to hear that you think she doesn't."

"No way," she said. "It's just so damn sad."

"It is at that," he said, "but we're not out of hope, as it hasn't happened yet."

She looked at him with a smile on her face. "If you need any help, count me in."

He looked at her a moment and then nodded. "Any idea what we can do?"

"No, I was hoping you did." Her hopes fell, as she realized he didn't know how to save Bernie either. "If you don't have any legal pull from the War Dog Division or the government," she said, "then I don't think anybody can do anything about her." She looked around and said honestly, "Sometimes I think, each time I'm here, that I should just steal her and run."

"If that was the answer," he said, "I'd do it too."

She nodded and frowned. "But we'd be seen," she said. "I don't know how many cameras they have on this place, but there's no way to do it without being seen."

"I hear you," he said quietly, gently stroking the dog's ears, as she stretched out on her side, her legs kicked out in front of her and her head on his thigh.

"She accepted you so fast," she murmured, studying him.

His smile was deep, gentle. "She knows I'm no threat. I'm still trying to figure out your sister's motivations," he said, "because that might be the easiest way to get this fixed."

"I think it's probably too far gone for that," she said. "And then my sister …" Addie stopped.

"Your sister what?"

She winced. "I …" Then she stopped again.

"You know I'll hear it all anyway, so it's probably easier if I hear it from you."

She shook her head. "There's no easy about it," she said. "I don't know quite what happened, but my sister and this dog did not get along right from the beginning. Bernie—the dog—didn't like Bernie, my sister, at all."

"Well, I happen to trust this dog's instincts more than I do people's," he said. "So what's wrong with your sister?"

She gave a bitter laugh. "So much," she said, "but one of

the biggest issues is she's just very selfish and very self-centered. And I know that's a terrible thing to say about my own sister, but it just seems like everything she's ever done was more about her. She's very high maintenance."

"A lot of women are," he said. "That doesn't make them bad people."

"No." Addie blew out a long hard sigh. "And I sound like I'm a jealous sister, and that's not what I mean at all," she said. And, of course, he didn't understand. Why would he? Besides, he was male, and she gave a bitter laugh, as he had yet to even meet her sister. Bernie was a stunner. Men fell for her all the time. It just blew Addie away that they could bypass all her personality issues and become enamored with what they thought they saw instead of what was really there.

"Do you think she held it against her that the dog didn't like her?"

"I know so, and she got to really hate her because everybody else loved her."

"So this was personal?"

"How can it be personal?" she asked in wonderment. "It's a dog."

"Was it a competition though?"

She stared at him, her brows crinkled. "Maybe," she said, "I guess if you want to look at it that way."

"Well, how else do you look at it?" he asked curiously.

She shrugged. "I don't know. It just seems a strange thing to say."

"Maybe," he said, "but it seems like we have a bite, supposedly a second and third bite, the injury bad enough that we have a doctor's report somewhere that we have to deal with. And because the owners themselves surrendered the dog and said that she's too dangerous for them to handle and that they want to put her down, there's nothing to stop this."

"Which is why I've been fighting so hard. My parents aren't even in town."

"And where are they?"

She winced because, of course, this would make her parents look stupid too. "They went on holiday."

He stared at her.

"I know," she said. "They don't handle this kind of stress very well."

"They applied for and adopted, after quite a process, a War Dog. This War Dog."

"I know," she said, "and, when it got here, they thought it would be a solution, but instead it became a problem."

"Did they get along with the dog?"

"Yes, actually they did. My dad likes her."

"And yet he was okay for her to be put down?"

"I don't think that was it as much as the fact that, once my sister got badly hurt, they were horrified and immediately wanted to be clear of the problem. And my dad is a strong proponent of animals, but only if they're kept properly. And, in this case, he believes that the War Dog was defective from the beginning, and it was a bad deal, so they needed to just get rid of it."

"Defective?" he asked in an ominous tone.

She shrugged. "I think he thought that it was injured in some way, and that's why it was being retired, and nobody told them the full facts, and they ended up with a dog that has a screw loose."

"Right," he said. He looked down at Bernie. "Does she look like she has a screw loose?"

"I never thought that," she said quietly.

"It's too bad you couldn't have looked after the dog," he said, eyeing her.

"Wouldn't that have been nice," she said, "but I wasn't given that option."

"And why is that?"

She shook her head.

"Wouldn't you have been a better answer than killing her?"

"No, because in my parents' world, they probably thought that I would just get bit too."

"I wonder though," he said. "It's possible, but, as I don't know what set it off in the first place, I don't know how to explain whether it would happen again or not."

"I don't think it would happen again," she said. "By the time my parents went for a holiday, my sister thoroughly hated the dog, and the poor thing's life was not great. I didn't know who I was supposed to complain to. I kept interfering, but I don't live at home, and my parents just had enough, and they left Bernie with Bernie. I don't know what happened after that."

"So there was a bad situation, which they couldn't handle, and they just walked?" he asked incredulously.

She looked at him, and then, not knowing what else to do, she answered with the truth. "Yes."

CHAPTER 2

"**I** GET THAT this probably makes my parents not seem very responsible," Addie said hesitantly, feeling disloyal again.

"It sounds like a recipe for disaster," he said shortly. "They brought an animal into this scenario, and they could easily have contacted the War Dog Division and returned her."

She thought about that and then said, "And I don't know why they didn't do that."

"Well, if they didn't have the guts to deal with your sister, they probably didn't want to admit that it was a mistake."

"Maybe," she said, hating to frame her parents in this exact way. "They're not bad people. They're just ... ineffective?" she said unhappily.

"Does that make it any better?"

"No," she said, "but the problem is, I don't know how to help the dog now. I didn't know how to help her back then either," she said, throwing out her hands. "I've hardly even slept since this happened. All my sister wants is for the dog to be dead, and it makes her happy every time I get upset about it."

"Because she wants to see you suffer?"

"Maybe," she said quietly, "that would be in line with

my sister."

"She sounds like a psychopath," he said in a short answer.

"Well, I hope not," she said, "because we do share blood, and I'd hate to think I was the same."

"I don't think sharing blood has anything to do with it," he said. "Sometimes people like that just don't care about anything but what they want, and they thrive on other people's wounds."

"Doesn't make her sound very nice at all," she said, hating the entire conversation. She stood and said, "Look. I don't want to talk about my family like this."

"No, you don't have to," he said, "but, if you've got anything inside you that wants to see this situation rectified," he said, "you need to help me get her out of here."

"And I said I would, but I was hoping you had a methodology that would work legally."

"Not sure yet," he said thoughtfully. "I need to talk to your sister."

She winced. "Do you have to?"

"She's the one who raised the complaint, so I'll say yes," he said. "I also need to get the full file. And, so far I'm not sure if anybody here will be cooperative, and I'll have to get some legal push to do that."

"I'd like to see the file myself," she admitted, "because I don't know what doctor she went to."

"Well, there have to be photographs, and there has to be a doctor's report about how bad the injury was," he said. "I'd like to see all that. In fact, I would like to see the wound now."

"I don't think you'll be seeing that at all," she snapped. "My sister will not show me, so she certainly won't show you."

"Who's looking after the bandage and draining the wound and taking care of all the medical stuff?" he asked, hopping to his feet.

She tilted her head, frowning. "What do you mean?"

"The wound's supposed to be bad," he said, "as in she was hospitalized or got stitches, as in somebody needs to be caring for it. Does she have a home care nurse? Does she go to the doctor? What is she doing?"

She stopped, stared, and then said, "I don't live with her, so I'm not exactly sure," she said cautiously. "But I don't remember hearing anything about it."

"So let me ask you point-blank," he said. "Does she even have a bite?"

She stared, hating that he was bringing out her worst fears. The one she'd flung at the neighbor. "Well ..." Then she froze. "I don't know," she said. "I've never seen it."

"What are the chances that your sister's just a liar, hating the dog, and delighted that it'll get put to sleep but needed to force it to be put to sleep, so created this whole mess as a fabrication?"

"It's possible," she said, "but I would hate to think so."

"Well, you might hate to think so," he said, "but I don't want to see an innocent dog go to its death because of a selfish vindictive woman with no boundaries."

And Addie knew that she'd taken a trip down a rabbit hole that wouldn't have an easy ending.

He reached down, gently stroked the top of Bernie's head, and said, "I'll be back, sweetie."

The dog barked at him once.

He nodded. "Let me see if I can get some legal paperwork done fast."

TUCKER QUICKLY TOOK several photos of Bernie, and, as he stood here, leaning against the cage, he sent off messages to Badger and his sister. The ones to Badger were all about paperwork. **We need legal backing, and we need help. It could be that the entire thing was faked. Need a copy of the doctor's file.**

Interesting came Badger's response. **We're on it, but, given the time frame, do what you can from there.**

As Tucker put away his phone, he stepped out and closed the gate, looked back at the dog, who stared at him with that fixed look in her eyes. "I'll be back, Bernie," he said. "Don't worry. We'll get you out of here."

He watched as Addie walked ahead of him. "I don't know about that," she said, wrapping her arms around herself. "It's just a shitty situation."

"With shitty people involved apparently."

She swallowed, knowing that she'd given such a horrible impression about her family, but, at the same time, she no longer knew what to believe. "If my sister did fabricate all this," she said, "can we save the dog's life?"

"If we can prove it was all fake, yes," he said, "but, in the meantime, we have almost no time to do anything."

"What about a stay order?"

"We could, but it depends on the manager here. He didn't seem too cooperative."

Out at the front reception desk, Wendy looked up, smiled at her, and said, "Oh, I see you two met each other."

"Yes," she said.

At that, he stepped forward and said, "I need a copy of the doctor's report."

Wendy stammered about.

"Call the manager back," Tucker demanded. "Please."

The sullen fat man returned, primed for this latest altercation. "What?"

"I want to see the doctor's report."

"What doctor's report?"

"You know what doctor's report. The one concerning the supposed bite Bernie Rottenheim got from the War Dog of the same name."

"It was … verbal."

"*Right.*" Tucker turned to the receptionist. "Do you have a business card?" he asked. "My lawyers need to contact you."

Wendy's smile fell away, and she handed him the boss's card, while shooting the manager a quick glance. "Is there a problem?" she asked Tucker.

"Absolutely there's a problem," he said. "That dog never bit anybody. Any report, verbal or written, on such an incident is a lie. And I intend to prove it." And, with that, he turned and walked outside. He could hear the two women talking a little bit, but he didn't give a damn. As soon as he stepped outside, his phone rang. It was Badger.

"So you need to tell me that again."

"Well, apparently the victim won't let her sister even see the wound. I need a copy of the file. I want to know what doctor sent in the report, and I need to know what I have to do to put a stop to this," he said. "Otherwise I'll make a social media scene that you've never seen before," he said, "because this dog did not do anything."

"We need the facts straight first," Badger said in a warning tone.

"Sure, but then we also need a copy of that file and

proof that the dog did bite someone. The guy here doesn't have a doctor's report and doesn't care, and the sister detested the dog and wanted to get rid of it. But she conned her parents into adopting it as the dog and she share the same name. The dog hated her right from the first day, and I believe the feeling is mutual."

"And what about the parents who adopted the dog?"

"Well, they don't handle the strife or the daughter well, so they took off on a holiday."

"Expecting all this to be over with before they get back, I presume?" Badger said in disgust.

"As far as I can tell, yes," Tucker said. "Honestly, it's all BS. I swear to God that dog's never done anything wrong in her life."

"Well, you need to hold that thought, but we'll have a bit of a fight to get that kill order canceled."

"Get it extended at least," he said.

"I'll do what I can," he said. "You need to track down the doctor, and you need to track down that sister and get a look at the leg."

"Yeah, I'm not sure how to do that. She's one of the most manipulative people going, and her whole goal is to get rid of the dog and to save face. She's getting a lot of attention from this."

"Great, she gets the attention, and the dog doesn't."

"Yeah, that's the way these people work, right? What we need to do is save the dog and figure out how to punish the daughter later. In the meantime, we need the War Dog out of here."

"I hear you. Is she in any danger? She should be well cared for," Badger said.

"She's in a cage, but I don't trust the manager of the

pound. I think he's been abusing Bernie. She regarded him as the enemy."

"Does he have any connection to the sister?"

"No clue, but it's something I'll have to look into," he said, "and that's depressing too."

"It sounds like another play of their game," he said.

"I think so. I just don't understand who, what, and why."

"You will," Badger said with confidence. "Don't worry. You will."

"I hope so. It's just shit right now, and I'm pretty damn pissed off about the whole thing."

"Good," Badger said. "Get pissed off, but don't get mad. Get even." He added, "If nobody else can give that dog justice, make sure that we find justice for her. She deserves it. She's saved a ton of military lives, and we need to make sure that we do the same for her."

TUCKER HUNG UP, and Addie joined him. "Let's go see your sister."

Addie grimaced.

"I want to see the wound and the doctor's report. Got any better ideas?"

"No, but my sister won't answer your questions, won't agree to show you anything," she said.

"Typical psychopath. Still needs to be done. Are you in, or are you out? Don't waste my time. I need to talk to your sister. Can you make that happen?"

She winced. "I can take you there," she said. "No guarantee that she'll talk to you." At that, her phone rang, and she looked down. "Speaking of which," she said, "it's my sister." She answered it. "Bernie, what's up?"

Tucker leaned in closer to overhear both sides of the conversation.

"I'm outta painkillers," she said petulantly.

"Did you check the bathroom?"

"Of course I did," she said.

"What about the upstairs bathroom?"

"Yes, I checked there too."

"Fine," she said. "I'm out shopping. I'll come by afterward."

"And fast," Bernie said.

Addie looked to see Tucker's eyebrows raised at that. "Yeah, I should be there in maybe fifteen minutes."

"Good. Damn dog," she said. "I didn't think it would take this long to heal from something like that."

"Maybe I should take a look at it when I'm there," she said. "Make sure it's not infected."

"No," her sister snapped immediately. "Nobody's fucking touching it."

"Well, when's your next doctor's appointment?" she asked.

"I don't have one. I'll be just fine without it," she said with a sneer. "I'll be much better when the dog's dead. On Friday. Then at least I know he won't come after me again."

"It's a her, not a him," she said, pinching the bridge of her nose.

"Whatever. It'll be dead soon. That's all I care about."

"If you say so," she said. "I'll come over in a bit." She hung up the phone. Of course he heard, but she repeated, "Bernie, asking for her painkillers."

"Yeah, she's a total psycho bitch. But those painkillers

were prescription, right?"

Addie nodded but frowned too. "Yeah?"

"Which will have a doctor's name on them. Good. That's easy enough to find. Let's go. I'll deal with your psycho sister then."

They arrived at the family home, and Addie let them in with her key. Her lazy self-entitled sister remained on the couch in the living room.

"About time. Get me my painkillers."

Addie winced, turned to Tucker.

He whispered, "Don't let her know I'm here yet. Get the pills. I need a snapshot of the doc's info."

Addie silently headed upstairs, where she had last seen the pills. Finding them, she brought them to Tucker.

"What the hell is taking you so long?" Bernie demanded.

Tucker took several photos of the painkillers, then pocketed them, calling the doc, who was quick to say he didn't treat any bite, mosquito or dog or snake bite or otherwise, for Bernie. Tucker hung up. "Introduce us now."

"Who the hell is that?" Bernie asked, when she noted the presence of the man with Addie.

Bernie wore long pants. In the summertime in Miami. *How convenient.* "I'm a representative acting on behalf of US Navy Commander Cross. I've come to see the supposed bite wound."

Bernie frowned, taking a sec to adjust to the new threat. "Get the hell out of here," she shrieked.

"After I see the wound and have a photo of it for the US Navy's file."

Bernie grabbed her phone. "I'm dialing 9-1-1."

Addie looked to Tucker, as if to ask, *Now what?*

Just wait, he mouthed. When he heard no sirens in three

minutes, he faced Bernie. "Now that we've confirmed you are a liar, want to try again? Show me the wound."

"Go to hell."

"See?" he said to Addie, as he continued loudly. "You've got yourself a full-fledged psychopath for a sister. She should permanently be in a psychiatric hospital, as she is harmful to others, if not to herself."

Bernie's shrieks grew louder and louder, as Tucker's smile grew bigger and bigger. He called Badger. Wanted Bernie to hear this. "The complainant is a psychopath and a liar. No proof of doctor's report. No evidence of wound. Call the major and the governor to demand the release of the War Dog. And file with Commander Cross a malicious report made to the US Navy by Bernie Rottenheim. Also ask for a seventy-two-hour hold on our lying complainant."

Badger laughed. "Good job. Stay on it. I'll work the angles from my end too."

Tucker and Addie left, Bernie's shrieks easily heard even as they walked down the driveway.

CHAPTER 3

A DDIE WALKED OVER to Tucker as he hopped into the
truck. "May I have your contact information please?"
she asked.

He looked at her in surprise, but then he saw the concern in her gaze. "For your sister's sake or for the dog's sake?"

"Look. I know my family is at fault for this," she said,
"but I can't be blamed for everything they do. I can only do
what I can to try and fix this. I want to save that dog as
much as you do."

He remembered the relationship between the two of
them—or at least appeared to because his gaze softened.
"Well, I did see the dog and how she reacted to you," he
said. "Honestly I would trust the dog's reaction over people's
any time."

"And I know that," she said, "and you don't have any
reason to trust me, but I love her. The dog, Bernie. Not so
much my sister, Bernie."

"And that was obvious," he said quietly. He pulled out
his phone and said, "Here's my number."

She keyed it into her phone and then gave hers to Tucker. "And I'm ... I'm sorry," she said. "I just ... I don't know
how to fix this."

"Well, I'm working on it," he said, shaking his head.
"Are you serious? That's your sister?"

She nodded slowly. "Like I said, it's a difficult situation."

"She doesn't care about the dog at all, does she?"

"Only that it dies," she said, "and that's what I'm up against daily. It's her whole focus."

"Do you have any idea how bad the bite supposedly is?"

"You tell me," she said. "I thought it had to be bad before the dog was put to sleep."

"It should be. How mobile is she?"

"Not," she said, "she stays on the couch all the time. She has a bedroom on the main floor anyway."

"And yet she says she went upstairs to check for her pain pills."

Addie stopped and stared. And then she nodded slowly. "Yes, she did say that."

"So really, could she have gotten up the stairs?"

"I don't know. I mean, if the bite's as bad as she says it is, then maybe not."

"If there was no bite, why does she need the pain pills?"

She shrugged. "I don't know."

"So why would she have you come and get them in the first place?"

"Attention? To yank my chain," she said shortly.

"Wow." He stopped and stared at her. "You have a truly messed-up family."

"I have a messed-up sister," she corrected. "I've admitted that. I don't want to keep harping on it."

"No, I got that," he said. "And I guess she won't let me see the bite either, unless I come back with a warrant and the cops." Tucker hesitated. "Maybe I'll have to do that anyway," he said.

She looked at him with interest. "Can you?"

He shrugged. "I'm not exactly sure what my legal backing is. Badger and I are sorting that out now."

"Isn't that …" Again she stopped and hesitated.

"What?"

"I don't know. I just would like to see some protection for the dog."

"A lot of places in the US don't give a damn about dogs," he said. "Animal protection, … animal rights are nonexistent, no matter how much legal jargon says otherwise."

"No. I was hoping Miami was a little bit better."

"Not once there are several accounts that this animal's dangerous—Bernie's account backed up by your parents."

"Her friend said it was dangerous too, said it bit her."

"Which friend is that?"

"Olive," she said.

"Do you have Olive's number?"

"Yeah," she said, "I think I do." She pulled out her phone, looked it up, and gave it to him. "What will you do?"

"I'll go interview her," he said. "See what she wants to say and if there's any legal standing behind this. Where her word is on record."

"Oh," she said. "I would love to be a fly on the wall with that," she said, "but Olive isn't exactly very fond of me."

"Well, I wonder why," he said with a brief laugh. "If she's a friend of your sister's, you know that anybody who isn't on your sister's side is against her. You're either my friend or you're my enemy in your sister's world."

"How do you know so much about her mental state?" she asked, staring at him. The fact that he was right was also kind of scary.

"Because I've studied people for a long time," he said. "It's also part of our training."

"What do you mean, training?"

"I was a Navy SEAL," he said briefly. "And one of the things that you must understand going into these missions is the psychology behind people, their behavior, and their motivations. I've met a couple people like your sister, not too many thankfully," he said. "But it usually involved bigger issues—kidnappings and government coups, all kinds of garbage like that," he said. "It hasn't come across my desk in this form before."

"But then you probably never dealt with something small like this, have you?" she asked.

He raised one eyebrow and then nodded. "That's quite true. I think I'll call this Olive and see if I can meet her."

"Do it now," she said. "See if she's even receptive to it. I can show you where she lives, but I can't guarantee you that she'll talk to you just because of me."

He pulled out his phone, quickly dialed the number Addie gave him, and he walked a few steps away. She heard him identify himself as Tucker Wilson. On behalf of the US Navy War Dogs Division. She loved that. As soon as he hung up, he turned back around and said, "She said she'll talk to me."

"Good. Where?"

"Not at home, she doesn't want to be there for the conversation," he said with a wry smile. "Yeah, I'm not surprised."

"Why?" Addie asked.

"Because home will also remind her very much of the girlfriend she defended, even though she may not have had any reason to. So I'll go find out," he said.

As he walked back to his driver's seat and hopped in, she asked, "Will you let me know the outcome of the meeting?"

He titled his head, studying her, and then said, "Maybe."

She frowned and added, "I *am* trying to save the dog. If Olive lied, and my sister's lying about all this, which it seems she has, once again," she said on a sigh, "I'll feel even worse."

"Well, if anybody lied about it, including Olive too," he said, "we need to make sure the animal is rescued, and then we go after the perpetrators of the lies because a lot of government time and energy was wasted protecting a War Dog that didn't need to be in the pound at all."

"Ouch," she said. "That scenario would cause a rift like you wouldn't believe in my family."

"Sounds like your family needs to be shaken up anyway," he said.

"I know. I know," she said. "It's just not that easy."

"Doing what's right is often not easy," he said, "but that's what makes it worth doing." And, with that, he drove away.

TUCKER WATCHED AS Addie pulled away from the family home, right behind him. The question was, would she follow him all the way to the coffee shop where he was due to meet Olive? That wouldn't surprise him either. The one thing that Addie had going for her was the dog's reaction to her arrival at the pound. The dog was overjoyed when Addie arrived. Already a bond was there, and that made his heart smile.

As for the sister, she was a Class A bitch. And he had zero interest in having anything more to do with her, other than institutionalizing her. The fact that she was orchestrating all this was one thing, but to consider that she was orchestrating it at out of hate was another thing entirely. And that would never be acceptable. Now he had to figure out how to stop it on this end, while Badger worked his magic on his end.

As Tucker drove, his phone rang. He put the phone on the dash carrier and punched Talk. "Hey, Rodney. All ready for the wedding?"

"Honestly? I would have canceled it if I had the chance," his soon-to-be brother-in-law said. "We've got that damn firebug going on here, and I can't get any help."

"I've got a dog here that was trained for fire sniffing with various accelerants," he said, "but she's on death row in the pound. Has until Friday."

"What!" He quickly asked, "Any chance we can get her on loan?"

"Well, you can bet, if I can get her out, she won't be going back," he said. "And we're working the angles right now to get her released, at least temporarily," he said. "We have to get the stay order extended first though, and so far we're running up against some roadblocks."

"If you want help from me," he said, "I do know the Governor. I can certainly put in a good word for her, if she can come help me out."

"Not only can she come help you but she can also quite likely tell what accelerant was used and if anybody in your crew or on your staff has been using it recently."

"Oh, Jesus," Rodney said, "I need her, and I need her now."

"Then you start making phone calls," he said. "I'll go see one of the women who said the dog was dangerous, and her testimony is partly why the dog is sitting in the pound, awaiting her death." He added, "And then I have a problem with the woman who was supposedly bitten by the dog but has this hate relationship with the War Dog, even though she's the one who begged to get it. I still don't understand her motivation on that part." He took precious moments to try to explain, ending up with, "I'm here now at the coffee shop," he said, as he pulled into the parking lot. "I'll contact you afterward to let you know what comes of this interview."

"Well, I won't wait for you to call me back," he said. "If that dog can help me, I need her here." And, with that, his soon-to-be brother-in-law hung up. Tucker smiled because Rodney and his sister had been together for a good ten years. They should have tied the knot a long time ago. But, for whatever reason, somebody was always putting it off to a better time, and, of course, that's what would have happened here again.

Tucker hopped from his truck, slightly distracted, only to smile when a car pulled in and parked on the other side. Addie might have thought she was hiding, but there was no hiding something like that. Ignoring Addie, who had followed him to the coffee shop, he headed inside, not knowing who he was meeting but hoping he could spot Olive somewhere.

When he saw a nervous woman sitting in front of the window, he ordered a coffee for himself, as he continued to study her, wondering how he could make this work on his behalf. He didn't have any legal backing for this job, not on paper anyway, but he was hired by Titanium Corp on behalf of US Navy Commander Cross to find this War dog and rescue her. And that was something he took seriously, especially in this case with her slated for death on Friday. So he was officially here. It's just he didn't have any written proof of it. It would all be determined by his attitude, as he played the tough guy. He had to because the dog's life was riding on it.

And, with his coffee, he walked over, stood at the edge of the table, looked down at her, and said, "Are you Olive?" His voice was hard, distinct.

She looked up, nervously spilling the coffee in the cup in her hand, and she nodded. "Yes. Yes," she said, "I am."

He nodded, sat right down across from her, and said, "So I need to hear from you exactly what happened."

"What do you mean?" she squeaked.

"You've said the dog was dangerous and attacked you several times."

"Well, he didn't, … she did attack me," she said.

He pulled out his phone, already on Record, and a notepad and started taking notes. She looked at the phone with a frown. He looked up and said, "I'm taking notes." He added, "And recording this."

Her eyes widened. "Recording it?"

"Yes, recording it," he said. "You must sign this statement, confirming you're telling the truth." He watched the color bleach from her face. And he stared at her hard. "You're not telling the truth, are you?" She gulped, looked at him, and then turned toward the window. "You do understand that a life is being taken because of your statement, correct?"

"But it's just a dog," she said, with a startled look.

"A dog that hundreds of thousands of military dollars have been put into for her training. That's a War Dog. An animal that went to war and saved thousands of military lives because of her training, and now you're saying that she's dangerous, too dangerous to be left alive. And so all that money and training will go down the tubes."

"But she's retired," she said, still trying to assimilate the information he had given her.

"No, she's needed at a job site not very far from here where there's a firebug," he said. "You do realize that's what she's trained for, right? Sniffing out accelerants and arson."

She swallowed again. "No, I didn't know," she said in a bare whisper.

"So we need to know the truth, the whole truth, and nothing but the truth. Do you want to start again?"

She swallowed hard and said, "I never really had anything to do with the dog."

He stopped, leaned back in his chair, and stared at her. "What did you just say?"

"I was scared of it," she said quietly, but almost so quietly he couldn't hear.

"You had nothing to do with this dog, and yet … you said in a written declaration that this animal was dangerous. Is that correct?"

She stared at him, her eyes huge, and then she gave a very small nod.

"I see," he said. "So what you're essentially saying is you lied." Her eyes widened, and he said, "Is that correct?"

And she slowly nodded again.

He shook his head and quickly sent a message to Badger. "I'm handing your name and phone number off to my boss," he said. "He'll get in touch with you about making a new legal statement, recanting your lies from the earlier one," he said.

"Unless … I don't want to deal with him, right?"

"No, not at all," he said. "However, not only did you lie," he said, "but a life is at stake, and we have to get all this rescinded before that dog is put to death."

"But ..." And then she fell silent.

He gave her a hard look. "But what?"

"What if I hadn't come here to meet you for coffee?" she said in a small voice.

"Do you really think I wouldn't have tracked you down to your house?" he said. He switched tabs on his phone and held up her address to show her.

She looked at it and squeaked.

"When you start lying at this level of lies," he said, "there are consequences. Did you not think about that?"

"She said that I wouldn't have to do anything."

"And who's that?" She fell silent. "You mean, your *best friend*, Bernie?" She looked up at him, her eyes wide. "Do you think I won't talk to her too?"

"Have you yet?"

"Of course I have," he said. "She was not happy with me. So you shouldn't be calling her and telling her about how you spilled the beans with me. You're aiding and abetting her in a lie, and you're already in enough trouble right now. At the moment it's probably forgivable. *If* we save the dog. But, if you continue on this pathway, then there could be criminal and civil charges."

"But it's just a dog."

He stopped and stared. "*Just* a dog?"

She swallowed hard. "Okay, so it's a fancy dog," she said, "but I didn't think there'd be any harm done. After she bit Bernie, I thought for sure the dog should be put down. So I just added a little to the story to make sure that they believed her."

"And was that done on your own or with Bernie's assistance?"

"Well, she told me that it wouldn't hurt, and then it

would help to make sure that this dog didn't hurt anybody else."

"Did you ever see the bite wound on Bernie?"

"No, of course not," she said with a wince and a shudder. "I can't stand to look at anything like that."

"So how do you know if she's been bitten?"

At that, she gave another squeak and stared at him, her mouth open.

"That's what I thought," he said. "You don't even know if she has or not, do you?"

"No," she said slowly. "I … I don't." She took a long slow deep breath. "Oh, my God, is she just doing this to get that dog killed?"

"Well, that'll be the question I ask next," he said. "Would she do something like that?"

She slowly nodded. "Yeah, she would. She hated that dog."

"And yet she insisted on getting it," he said.

"But the dog didn't like her," she said. "It was obvious the dog didn't like her."

"I wonder why."

She shrugged. "She didn't treat it very well. I told her that she shouldn't treat it so badly, but she said that it was just a dog and that it didn't matter."

"How badly did she treat her?"

"It would be sleeping on the floor, and she'd come up and hit it with something hard, like with the leg of a chair, and it would jump back, growling at her all the time."

"But, of course, she never did that when anybody else was around, did she?"

"No, she never did."

"I'm surprised the dog didn't attack her and rip her leg

off for that kind of behavior," he said. "What else did she do to the dog?"

"She would feed the dog and then chase her away when it was half done and take the food and dump it and wouldn't feed her again for another couple days. Or she'd pour stuff on top of it that wasn't any good for the dog, like dish soap. And then she wouldn't let the dog out to go to the bathroom, and it would shit everywhere and then ..." And she stopped. She shook her head. "She didn't treat it very nice."

"So, even if it did bite her, what would you say to that now?"

"She probably deserved it," she said, "but, I mean, all dogs are bad. I mean, I'm scared of all of them."

"So, because you're scared, they're bad?"

"Well, no." She stopped and said, "I was bitten when I was little." She added, "So I'm just really, really scared of them."

"Did this dog deserve anything that your friend did to it?"

"No," she said, "she was just ..." And then she stopped again. "Honestly she's not a very nice person."

"And yet she's still your friend?"

"Well, I don't have many friends," she said, "and she's not somebody that you become *unfriends* with."

"What do you mean by that?"

"Well, you're only *not friends* when she decides you're not friends. It's not like I can turn around and tell her that I don't want to be with her anymore."

"You sure about that?" he asked. "Because it sounds like it would be to your benefit to find other friends."

"I don't have any," she said, "so I don't really have a choice."

"Yes, you do," he said, staring at her, his brows pulling together, as he wondered at that kind of dependency in a really ugly relationship. "What do you get out of the relationship?"

She just stared at him.

"You get out of it the fact that you're not alone," he said, "and I get that, but you need something more to be fully living your life too."

"You don't understand," she said.

"I understand more than you think," he said. "The bottom line is, it's still not a healthy relationship if you're only there because you can't get out of it."

"Well, she's my friend," she protested.

"Your *friend* told you to lie, and now you're next in the line for the lies that you said based on her advice. Over something that she's lied about too," he said calmly.

She just stared at him and said, "I need to talk to her."

"Well, I wouldn't do that now that I've talked to her and now you," he warned, "because that'll be a whole different ball game with her once you do."

She sank back. "I ... I just don't even know what to do right now," she said, nervously pulling her purse closer and looking like she was ready to run.

"Well, you tell me," he said. "What do you think you should do?"

"I'd like to go home and have a shower," she said. "I feel icky all of a sudden."

"Can you go home and not call her, or will you feel compelled to call her and to let her know all about our conversation?" he said in disgust.

"Well ..." Then she stopped and shook her head. "No, I won't call her," she said. "She'll rip into me pretty badly for it."

"And why is that?"

"Because absolutely no way am I ever supposed to have told you about this."

"You didn't," he said. "I already knew."

She looked at him intently and then nodded slowly. "And that might help me," she said.

"Besides, even if you did tell her, what would she do?"

"I don't know," she said in a whisper, "but I don't want to find out either." She looked up, shamefaced. "She can be mean."

"So you go home," he said. "Don't contact her." And then he lowered his voice, until it was soft and gentle. "Now I want you to think about other ways that you could find friends, who are true friends, who you want to have healthy two-way relationships with, who you wouldn't be ashamed of knowing." He added, "She lied. She's tried to cheat the system to put an animal, … an innocent animal, to death," he said. "There will be fallout, and you don't want to be associated with it any more than you already are."

She winced and shuffled closer toward the edge of her seat. "I still don't have any way to get to know people," she said, "and being alone sucks."

"But being alone is way better than being associated with somebody like her," he said quietly. "You need to come to some understanding of just what you have to offer in a friendship and find another way to make some friends. Maybe volunteer somewhere, do something that makes your heart smile—like taking an art class or a cooking class or something—instead of being with people who make you cringe," he said, "especially right now when she finds out that you have recanted your statement."

She looked at him and said, "But you only have my word for it."

He picked up his phone and said, "I recorded it. Remember?"

She stared at him in shock, bolted to her feet, and ran from the coffee shop. Of course she would try and recant her confession to him. People were like that. They would tell you the truth until it came back on them. And then they didn't want to have anything to do with it. He finished his coffee, got up, and slowly walked outside. And he was not at all surprised to see Addie waiting for him at his truck.

"And?" she asked.

"Olive was never attacked, never had any exposure to the War Dog, but she did say how badly your sister treated the dog, including getting blindsided by chair legs and stealing her dog food and then even adding dish soap to the food available to her." He watched her face as she heard his words.

"Oh, my God," she said. "Seriously?"

He nodded. "Yes, and I've got it on tape."

She shook her head. "I had no idea," she said. "That poor dog."

"Sounds to me like Bernie's suffered enough," he said. "I've got things in motion. I just have to make sure that the manager at the pound does not take things into his own hands."

"I don't know if we can trust him," she said. "I think he's an old friend of Bernie's."

"That's not good," he said. "I'll head back there right now."

"I'm coming with you," she said. "I can't take that chance."

"Yeah, I don't want to take the chance either," he said.

"Hopefully, while I'm there, I'll get word on her fate."

"I hope so." She looked at him and said, "I don't trust him."

"Neither do I," he said. He hopped into the truck and said, "I'll meet you there." He reversed out of the parking lot and headed back to the pound. As he drove, his brother-in-law called him and said, "The governor's making phone calls."

"Good," he said, "let's hope it's fast enough. I've just been told that the pound manager and the woman who put in the false complaints on the dog are friends."

"Jesus," he said, "make sure you get there and save that dog."

"Oh, I'd like to," he said, "but I need something official."

"I'm calling the governor back." Rodney hung up the phone.

Tucker pulled into the pound, racing up to the front. The receptionist looked at him in surprise. "You back again?"

"Yes, I need to see the dog."

Right behind him, Addie came in too. Wendy looked at her and then at the two of them and whispered, "I think she's being put to sleep right now."

"Buzz us through," Addie said. "Come on. Hurry, hurry, hurry." Wendy buzzed the door, and the two of them raced down the hallway to see the manager standing with the gate open, trying to get a hold of the shepherd backed into the corner and growling at him.

"Stop," Tucker called out.

The manager looked at him and said, "What the hell are you doing here?"

"You need to go answer your damn phone," he said. "The governor's calling."

At that, he stopped and stared. "What are you talking about?"

"This dog's not being put down," he said. "That's what I'm talking about, and nice try on moving the date forward."

"Hey, we have to pay bills too. I can't afford to feed her right now," he said.

"Not an issue anymore." He slipped past him, stepped into the cage in front of the dog. "She leaves here with me now," he said. "So you can take this up with the governor on the phone," he said. "Otherwise you've got a fight right now on your hands. If that's what you want, go for it," he said. And he stopped and waited.

CHAPTER 4

"I WOULD LISTEN to him, if I were you," Addie said from behind the manager.

He turned and glared at her. "Neither one of you are taking this dog until I know for sure what the hell is going on," he snapped. "The dog is a menace."

"The dog is not your problem," Tucker snapped back.

He glared at him. "Says you." And he stormed off.

Tucker looked down at the dog and said, "So will you behave yourself without a leash, or do I need a collar and a leash for you?" He snapped his fingers and said, "Heel."

Immediately she stood up, walked around, and came to stand at his side.

He gave her the second order. "Sit." Immediately her butt smacked down hard on the floor. "Now," he said, looking over at Addie, "we need to get this dog out of here."

"Well, it'd be nice to think we'd go out the back, but it'll be locked," she said.

"I have no intention of going anywhere but out the front." And, with the dog at his side, staying close under his orders, they walked out to the front area.

Wendy took one look, opened her mouth, and Tucker said, "Don't even start with me. He's on the phone to the governor right now, and the governor's got more than enough to say about this expensive dog being put to death for a trumped-up charge."

Wendy's mouth snapped shut, and her gaze widened. She looked over at the connecting door and said, "I have to get his permission."

"You do that," he said. "You've got about three seconds." And he stood here with his arms crossed, the dog waiting at his side.

Wendy got up and bolted into the other room. She came back a few seconds later, and she just held out her hands and said, "I guess you can go." She sounded completely bewildered.

"Yeah, I guess so," he said. "And when his little girlfriend phones him to see if the dog was put to sleep, tell him I'm on her case too. There will be charges on her end after this."

Wendy's gaze went to Addie, then back to him again. "Are you talking about Bernie?"

"Yes," he said, "liars and cheats don't get away with this kind of stuff. An innocent life was almost taken today."

"But ... the dog bit her," Wendy wailed.

"No," he said, "I spoke with her doctor who confirmed Bernie was lying."

At that, Wendy sat down hard and just stared at him.

He didn't give her a chance to say anything. He turned and walked out.

Addie walked over to Wendy and said, "I'm sorry this is such a mess."

"But are you serious?"

She nodded. "We haven't gotten to the bottom of everything at the moment," she said, "but the dog is a trained arson dog, and she needs to go out to a fire scene that matters to the governor."

"Jesus," she said. "You stay safe, huh?"

"Yes, and don't call my sister," she said. "Enough people are in trouble already."

Wendy swallowed hard and said, "How did you know?"

"I know," she said, "that she has this ability to make people do what she wants them to do and that they're the ones who always get in trouble."

Wendy turned and looked back at the door where the boss was and looked up at her. "He's involved too."

"I know, and you can bet that Tucker will make sure your boss gets in trouble too," she said, nodding toward the front door where Tucker had disappeared.

"Bernie and the boss were friends in high school. You can't tell it by looking at him now, but he was the quarterback."

"Won't matter. Tucker won't take any of this kindly. He'll have your jobs, and he'll have your heads on a platter, if he gets his way."

Wendy shrieked. "I can't afford to lose my job."

"Then keep your head down," Addie advised her, "and stay out of trouble. Enough is going around right now." And, with that, she turned and headed outside. As she got out there, Tucker already had the dog in the front of the truck, and he was starting to reverse. She hopped up to the driver's side window and said, "Wait."

He looked at her impatiently.

"You can't just do that and take off," she said in exasperation.

He grinned. "Why not? I got what I came for."

"Great," she said with an eye roll. "That's not helping me any."

"No, but it's helping the dog a whole lot," he said. "That

should make you happy."

"It does," she said, "but I also have to deal with my sister."

"Tell your sister that I'll deal with her," he said in an ominous tone.

She winced. "Threats? Really?"

"Look. Your family's been on mute for too long. Time someone spoke up. And I'm mad enough to speak the truth and to take the heat from your psycho sister. I could be nicer," he said, "but can't say I'm feeling that way right now."

"I don't have anything to do today," she said, hesitating, then burst out with, "Can I come with you?"

He stared her a moment, looked down at Bernie, and asked, "What do you think, Bernie? Should Addie come with us?"

Bernie barked at both of them. Tucker laughed and said, "Well, I have to be back tonight anyway, so if you're sure?"

"I'm sure," she said, not really knowing why but determined to go. "However, I don't want to leave my car here. They lock the fence around the pound at night. My place is not too far."

"Drive home," he said. "I'll follow behind and pick you up. Then we're heading to the condo complex where the fire was."

"Good," she said. "I want to see what the dog can do."

And, with that, she raced back to her car, hopped in, and this time he followed her as she drove the short distance to her residence. She hopped out, grabbed her purse, and waited for him to pull up alongside. She hopped into the front seat, Bernie giving her a joyful greeting. Addie laughed and chuckled as she hugged Bernie and said, "Oh, my goodness. It's so good to see you outta there."

"What did you tell Wendy?"

"I told her to not get involved any more than she needed to because there would be hell to pay over this."

"She's involved too, isn't she?"

"So is her boss—the high school quarterback, if you can believe it."

"Not," Tucker said, shaking his head.

"But he and Wendy are involved due to my sister's shenanigans."

"Isn't that enough?" he said, and his tone booked no argument.

"Yes, and no," she said. "I've seen it happen time and time again. They're only guilty of being my sister's friend."

"Your sister's guilty of a hell of a lot more," he said, his voice hard.

"Absolutely," she said, "but I still don't want you to punish her too badly."

"She needs it."

"Yes, she does," she said, "but whatever you do, it comes back on me, and it comes back on my parents." She sighed loudly, getting a worried look from Bernie. Addie smiled and petted the dog, soothing her. Bernie settled down immediately.

"They're another group who needs to be dealt with."

"What can you do to them?" she asked curiously. "I've been trying to get them to wake up and to see what she's like for a long time."

"They know," he said. "That's why they keep disappearing."

"Sure, but they don't know how to deal with it," she said sadly. "They can't do confrontations."

"That's never an answer with a child. Especially one who has learned how to control those around her and not in a nice way."

"She's hardly a child anymore," she said sadly.

"Yet you keep defending her."

"I don't want to," she said, "but it's not my problem either. And I know that sounds like a cop-out, but she's my younger sister. What else was I supposed to do all these years?"

"Stop babying her?"

"I moved out at eighteen because I couldn't stand it," she said, "and my parents only got worse."

"And it's probably gotten worse because you were part of keeping Bernie in check."

"Yes, that's true, but everything I tried to do was overridden by them. And they're the parents," she said. "What was I supposed to do?" That summed up the last five years of her life with her sister. Total frustration.

"Somebody needs to have a talk with them. Some professional mental health care provider."

"I don't know what they'll do, and that's their problem," she said. "Now that the dog's out and safe, my sister will be livid. I probably won't have anything to do with any of them."

"Really?" He looked over at her with a frown, patting Bernie softly with a free hand. She seemed to be sleeping.

"I haven't had much to do with them lately anyway," she said quietly. "Bernie's always been the apple of their eye, and I've always been the odd one out." She shrugged. "And that's okay too because I didn't want to end up like her."

"God, no," he said vehemently.

She laughed. "It's so funny being in a situation like this," she said. "You try so hard, and then you just have to walk away because, well, it's your family, but it's not *your* family. I can't force them to make the decisions I want them to make."

"And what do you do for work?"

"I'm a nurse," she said. "I'm on days off right now."

"Good for you," he said with a smile.

"What will you do now?"

"Meaning?"

"I'm not sure just who and what you are right now, but, outside of this job with the dog, do you go home now that the dog's safe, or do you find another home for her? What happens?"

"It's hard to say yet," he said. "I'm here in Florida for my sister's wedding as well, and that's nothing I'm looking forward to."

"Why not?"

"I just don't like all the pomp and ceremony that goes with it," he said with a shrug, "but I do love my sister so ..."

"So you'll go." She smiled at the thought of this big raw alpha male at a fancy wedding.

"And I'm slated to walk her down the aisle," he said. "It won't be such a huge wedding, so, well, whatever," he said. "A few minutes pain for a lot of gain on her part."

"Do you like her future husband?"

"Very much," he said, "and they've been together ten years. He's the one who's got the firebug event happening, and I'm heading there right now."

"Oh, good," she said. "That sounds like a close-knit family. I'm happy for you. I always wanted that but didn't get that."

"It's good at times. Then not really," he said. "When I

had my accident, and I was pretty close to not making it, she came and his family all came and clustered around me. Except I wanted the opposite. When I get hurt, I want everybody to leave me alone. But my sister, when she gets hurt, she wants lots of attention, lots of people around her."

"Two different types. My sister would be more like yours, and I'm more like you," she said. "I think there's also a happy medium, if people can get there."

He laughed. "Maybe," he said, "but, ever since then, I haven't let anybody come too close. I can't stand being overwhelmed."

"And maybe that's just because a lot of love is going on around you, but you're not comfortable receiving it."

"Whatever," he said with a wide grin. "That sounds like a lot of mumbo-jumbo hokeypokey stuff."

She laughed out loud. "Says the guy who went after anything and everything he could to rescue a dog. So righting wrongs matter, as does saving a life, one you've already lost your heart to."

"Of course. The dog deserved it," he said. "I'm not the greatest fan of people, but I do love animals."

And that adorable grin of his peeked out again. "Don't tell me. Was it human error that caused your accident?"

"They called it friendly fire," he said with a note of bitterness. "That's what happens when you work with allies, but they're not all vetted as closely as you would like to see them vetted."

"I'm sorry," she said. "You appear to be in good physical shape."

"I'm in as good a physical shape as I'll get," he corrected. "And that's a very different story."

"Ah," she said. "Well, let's hope that your recovery to

now is good enough."

"Has to be," he said, "because it is what it is."

She nodded and stayed quiet. "I've seen a lot of injuries in my career as a nurse," she said. "The human spirit has always amazed me at how much people can come back from."

"I didn't think I would come back from anything," he said quietly. "When you hear the noise from the gunfire going on around you, and you know it's bad, you don't expect to wake up. And then, in my case, wake up missing my lower leg with messed up knees, plus missing a ton of muscle and ..." He shrugged. "It's just ... the litany goes on and on," he said. "When you wake up—alive but missing parts—it's a shock," he murmured, "and that's not even the right word for it."

"No," she said. "It's not even close, is it? But you know something? ... You're blessed that you have recovered to the extent you have."

"And I know it," he said, glancing at her. "Don't worry. I'm very appreciative of all the effort that was put into keeping me alive, and I'll do all my best that I can to make the most out of what I have. But I'm certainly not delusional into thinking that what I have is what I had."

"No," she said, "but hopefully it's better."

STARTLED, HE LOOKED over at her and then gave her a slow dawning smile of appreciation. "Maybe," he said, "yeah, maybe."

He looked at her once more and saw her. Like, *really* saw her. The intelligence in her dark brown eyes, the softness to her expression, the gentle turn of her lips, the hair brushed off her forehead in an unconscious gesture that had nothing to do with fashion and all to do with comfort. Something was so natural and honest about her. Life had been such a rush since he'd gotten here that he hadn't even had a chance to stop and see who she was. He had blindly accepted her role in this as just Bernie's sister, and yet he had somehow agreed to let her come with him and the War Dog.

He looked at her again, shook his head, and said, "You're really cute. You know that?"

"What?" she asked, startled. "Where did that come from?"

He laughed. "Yeah, not my normal style either, but I was just thinking to myself that I've been so busy, so focused on saving this dog, that I hadn't seen you for who you are, outside of your family."

"I'm not sure anybody ever does. I've always been in my sister's shadow." At his snort, she said, "You met my sister."

"That I did. Not too interested in seeing her ever again," he said. "I know who she is on the inside. That's enough for me. Pretty is only skin deep. Ugly goes all the way through."

"Doesn't seem to matter to a lot of people," she said, studying him.

He glanced at her, caught her gaze, and smiled when he saw the flush on her cheeks. "I don't care about other people," he said. "I will go by a dog's barometer before I'll go by a human's. Dogs know instinctively who's good and who's bad, and they have a tendency to stay away from those who aren't any good. And your sister is evil."

"I know, but she's my sister. I don't know that she's *that* bad. I think she's just spoiled, entitled, lazy. But evil? I don't know."

Tucker shook his head. "Nope. No way I'm wrong about her. That's just you projecting your goodness on that hellhole who is your sister."

She stared at him. Not shocked but assimilating. "I hope not, but I haven't seen her in a good light in a long time," she said with a shrug.

"Well, your parents have created a monster, and that monster's their problem. They don't get to foist it off on the world because they don't want to deal with it."

"I think a lot of parents out there are in the same boat," she said quietly. "And I get that, for you, my sister has no redeeming factors, but she does. Everybody does."

"Maybe," he said, "but it'll take a long cold winter in hell before I'll see it."

"Because everything to you is black-and-white?"

"Absolutely not. It used to be, but it's not," he said. "It's all about how you look after the animals of the world, the innocent victims, children as well," he amended. "You can't just choose to look after only yourself. The world isn't like that."

"Or the world is exactly that," she argued.

"But it shouldn't be," he said. He looked at her to see her nodding.

"No, it shouldn't be," she said, "but too often it is."

"And you've seen some of the ugliness of human nature in your job too, haven't you?"

"Too, too much," she said. "I used to be an ER nurse, and I just ... I couldn't handle a lot of it, so I switched into a general practice, and now I work at a doctor's office."

"Nothing wrong with that either," he said.

"Nothing wrong with it, just a very different pace to what I was used to," she said with a half smile. "And now, of course, it's a lot calmer and a lot less trauma."

"Yes," he said, nodding. "I used to do missions where governments were being taken over and kidnappings were happening, and then, you know, boats were being boarded and passengers shot for the little bit of jewelry they had." He shook his head, then continued. "In some parts of the world, life is tough, and it's hard to make a living, but, more than that, it's all about themselves. It's all about doing what they want to do instead of what's right for everyone. Makes living a little bit harder for all of us."

"Is that the kind of work you used to do?"

"Yes," he said, "and I would be in that job for the rest of my life if I'd had a choice. Of course, most SEALs retire after eight to ten years. It's too hard on our physical bodies. However, I'm proud of the years of service I gave my country," he said, "and I don't begrudge the injuries I have from that. It's just frustrating that it was 'friendly fire.'"

"I'm not even sure how one explains that," she said. "I've heard the term several times, but I can't imagine the sense of betrayal."

"Still," he said, "it is what I have yet to deal with, so it doesn't matter how I feel about it. I've got to deal with it eventually."

"And, of course, dealing with it isn't just a case of saying, *I've dealt with it*. It's so much more," she murmured.

"Yep."

"Did you ever see a therapist for help?"

"Absolutely," he said, "a lot of people. Sometimes you have to go through a couple to find ones who work with you and work for you," he said.

"I can see that," she said. "I saw somebody when I was a teenager because I couldn't handle my sister."

He gave a snort at that. "I am not surprised," he said. "She is more than a handful."

"Back at the time I was dealing with all those insecurity issues too. Nothing like puberty to make a mess of your life," she said with a grin.

"Well, I hope you sorted that out."

"I did," she said. "It was a matter of deciding who was responsible for the mess that she was, and it wasn't me, so that made it a lot easier for me to walk away."

"Absolutely," he said.

She looked around and asked, "How much longer is the drive to the apartment complex?"

"It's a long way off. At least an hour more still. I guess I should have told you that first."

CHAPTER 5

"IT DOESN'T MATTER," Addie said, settling in. "I'm just happy to not be sitting at home, hating my sister and my life."

"Nope," he said, "you're on a pathway with a dog that's just been freed from certain death, and we're off to do good works." They both checked out Bernie, smiling to find her peacefully dozing.

"I like the sound of that. It's one of the reasons I went into nursing," she said. "I wanted to help people. I wanted to do something to help others. I didn't want to get stuck in that rut of being only caught up in the 'poor me' cycle."

"When you're raised with it all around you," he said, "I think you do two things. You either get sucked into it, and you become a mini-me, or you get to the point where you look around and say, 'That's not what I want for my life,' and you find a way out."

"Well, I found a way out, but then I found trauma nursing very difficult to handle."

"That doesn't mean it's a failure on your part," he said.

She shook her head. "I didn't expect you to pick up on that."

"It's amazing what we think of as failures," he said, "because I did the same thing after my accident. I figured it was my fault that I'd gotten shot. And, of course, nobody would even listen to that theory because it was garbage. Of course it was garbage. I wasn't responsible, and I wasn't at fault for having taken a bullet. But I felt like I'd let everybody else down, let my team down, because I couldn't be there for them anymore."

"Survivor guilt," she murmured. "Or just plain guilt. Seems like, if we don't have a reason to rack ourselves up and down over these things, we create a reason."

"Isn't that the truth," he said with a grin.

"See? We have a lot in common," she said, slowly liking him more and more. Of course she loved him for saving Bernie—the dog—right at the beginning. Being decisive with a take-charge attitude also appealed in a big way.

"We do," he said, nodding.

She looked over at him. "Where have you been staying before you came here for the dog?"

"I was in New Mexico, in Santa Fe," he said with a bright smile, "with friends of mine." And he explained about Badger and Badger's team.

"Wow," she said, "that is a nice thing to hear. The fact that they are still friends after all that and the fact that they've rebuilt their lives, giving purpose to it, that's huge."

"It is," he said, "and we often forget that they did it themselves. So we have to give them credit for all that as well."

Their trip was completed a few minutes later, as Tucker followed the GPS's directions, and they pulled into the parking lot to see a man standing outside his white truck, waiting for them. "That's my soon-to-be brother-in-law, Rodney," Tucker murmured.

They hopped out, and she came around to Tucker's side, eyeing the tall sandy-haired man with a bridge of freckles.

He grinned at the sight of Addie and held out his hand to shake hers. Tucker made the introductions, then stepped back and brought Bernie forward.

Rodney crouched in front of Bernie, held out his hand. She was very well mannered, sniffed his hand, her tail wagging; then she looked up and nudged his hand with her nose. "So this is the dog that we're talking about?"

"Yep, she was trained for fire, arson, bombs as well," Tucker said.

"Well, let's hope no bombs are here," Rodney said. "But I'll take all the help I can get. I can't keep this up."

"No, it's usually a simple case for the dog," he said. "How many crewmembers do you have here right now?"

"Too many and they're all looking for paychecks," he said with feeling.

"Well, take me first to the arson scene," Tucker said. "Then we'll talk."

"I want to watch you and the dog work," Rodney said.

"That's fine. The only thing is, I don't know if Bernie will take it as a distraction, once we get to the fire site," Tucker said, pointing to the dog. "And the fewer distractions, the better, since the dog is well trained, but I'm not."

Rodney hesitated and nodded. "I'll stay in the background." He looked at Addie. "Are you going?"

"Absolutely," she said. And she walked up to Tucker's side. "You don't have a problem with me coming, do you?"

He hitched out his elbow, and she tucked her hand in because it felt right, and Rodney led the two of them to the respective building. She didn't know who this Tucker guy was, but she knew she wanted to get to know him a whole lot more than she had. She knew Rodney eyed them speculatively too, figuring out just what their relationship was, and she was okay with that. Because, if he figured it out, he was doing better than they were. And, with that, they walked into the building.

A few feet inside, Tucker stopped, and both the dog and Addie stood beside him and stared. "Interesting fire pattern," he murmured, staring at the skeleton remains around them.

Rodney behind him said, "Exactly, right?"

"It's concentrated in the far corner of basically this unfinished portion of this building," he said. "You haven't got a roof on this one yet."

"I know, so the damage is a whole lot less here, but structurally all these trusses have to be replaced." Rodney pointed up to where some of the fire had charred the wood.

"And yet," Tucker suggested, "it could have been so much worse."

"Which begs the question as to whether the firebug had intentionally set this to do minimal damage or if he's just not good at this."

"A first-time firebug? Yeah, could be," Tucker added. He stopped to look at his brother-in-law and asked, "Have you been threatened at all?"

The question completely took the color right out of Rodney's face. He stared at Tucker in shock. "How did you know that?"

"Because this would be the next step," Tucker said. "So why don't you start from the beginning and tell me what's going on."

"I don't even know what's going on," he said in frustration. "It makes no sense. A couple months ago I started getting some protestors, people blockading us, not letting us drive in, all about this construction here. We've got all the permits. We did all our due diligence, and everything's clear to go."

"So it's locals?"

"Well, certainly a lot of locals seemed pissed off about it, but nobody would give us a reason as to why, not a legal one. Just that they didn't want this condominium complex here. They wanted to keep their pristine land unobstructed and don't want the community to get any bigger."

"Which is an old story," Addie said. "It's beautiful around here. I can see, if I had lived here all my life, how I probably wouldn't want to see growth and commerce coming in either."

"It's also a very poor area," Rodney said, "and everybody has to commute a long way for work."

"Which is what people moving in have to do as well, correct?" Addie asked.

"Yes," he said, "it'll add to the sleeping community feel of the place, but very little affordable housing is in town, and, because this is out of town, it will be that much more affordable."

"Was this a popular hiking trail or something like that?" she asked, Tucker listening in.

"Not really," Rodney said. "However, it was one of the original homesteads. We bought it for a song because the heir apparent just wanted his cash."

"Maybe if the locals knew that," Tucker said, "it would make them more upset."

"Maybe, but that's hardly our fault that he went ahead to sell it, is it?"

"No, of course it isn't, but you also know that emotions run strong and deep when it comes to things like this."

"I do know," he said. "I thought all their other arguments were thin. We couldn't find anything that was reasonable in any of their complaints."

"It doesn't have to be reasonable," Tucker said. "It's more emotional than that. You're a property developer, and generally you're looking at the bottom line, whereas they're looking at all the intangible reasons why this building shouldn't go up here. But back to the real issue, other than their original threat, what other threats have you had?"

"Well, a lot of letter-writing, contacting the various layers of government, little bits and pieces that we've dealt with many times at other projects. Then I started getting these weird letters left on my vehicle," he said. "They all seemed to be the same. They're cut-from-the-newspaper type notes, and they all say 'Stop work on this project.' No reason given. Nothing. Just *stop*. I have a whole bunch of them in my vehicle."

"So obviously somebody local. And I'll want to take a look at them afterward," Tucker said. "Did you contact the cops?"

"I did," he said immediately, "but they didn't seem to be too bothered."

"Now that arson's involved, how do they feel about it?"

"The cops said this was an accident," he said, "which is why I wasn't connecting the two events. But then I called in the fire inspector."

"Well, it's obviously not an accident," Tucker said. "The question is why."

"What? Why burn it? Why try to stop the building?"

"Both," Tucker said. "I get that they probably got so frustrated by following the legal routes that they realized maybe, if they could bankrupt you, then the building would just follow and lie here unfinished."

"Is that any better?" Rodney said starkly. "I mean, look

at it. It's not very pretty."

"But it's off the highway, and it does give whoever's doing this a certain sense of power that he managed to stop something. A lot of times people feel very ineffectual because they feel small compared to corporations or government, and they don't think they can do anything—which is true to a certain extent—but, at the same time, once they do take that next step and burn something down, they need bigger projects because they need to have that sense of accomplishment all the time."

"I don't like the sound of any of that," Rodney said.

"And that's not the issue right now either," Tucker acknowledged. "What we must sort out is, what will we do about it?"

"I don't think we *can* do anything," he said. "I mean, look at the place. I've got an insurance investigator out here already too, doing a full walk-through, and he did call me and admit that he thought it was arson."

"Who is it?"

"I don't know," Rodney said. "He's from out of state. The insurance adjuster sent him."

"No fire inspection here locally?"

"Coming soon, but the insurance companies wanted their person out here."

"And if the insurance doesn't cover it, then what?"

Rodney swallowed visibly. "Well, that would not be very good news. Matter of fact, that would be really ugly news for me."

"Enough to shut you down?"

He thought about it and said, "I'd have to find some new investment money," he admitted. "Which means, at the end of the day, less money for me, if there'll be any at this point," he said, "because I have to pay the workers in order to keep them. Otherwise they'll find new jobs, and, when I get back to work again, I can't find anybody."

"You don't contract for the job?"

"Well, I do, but, if the job has to stop, what am I supposed to do with my crew? And what are they supposed to do?" he said. "Everybody has to get paid. I can hardly blame them for taking on other work."

"I get it," Tucker said with a smile. "It'll be interesting getting to the bottom of this one."

"I'm not sure there's any bottom to get to though," he said. "Seriously the cops didn't seem to be too bothered."

"And mostly because the cops probably don't see it as arson. But the insurance investigator should be contacting them about that."

"Maybe. He didn't seem to care either. Neither did he give me a definite answer."

"Oh, he'll care the most, as they have to pay for the damages. So he's looking for any way to make this something that's not covered and their liability."

"Well, I am covered for arson," he said. "These kinds of ventures are too expensive. I can't underwrite everything." He shook his head in frustration. "It's crappy timing with the wedding and all."

"But it doesn't affect the wedding, does it?"

"No, not really, just frustrating." Rodney looked down at the dog. "What can she do?"

"I'm not sure yet," he said. "I need to walk her around. Certain commands start her working, and other commands keep her working, but she's been out of practice, and I don't know all the commands," he admitted. "It was still worth a try bringing her."

"What do you want me to do?" Addie asked.

"JUST STAY OUT of the way and don't distract Bernie," Tucker said, not sure how this would work. Bernie was looking at him for guidance, but he had little to give. "I'll walk her around and see if I can get her to signal anything."

"I'll go back with Rodney," she said, and Addie released Tucker's arm and stepped back. She and Rodney stopped at the front entrance. Tucker reached down and murmured something to Bernie that Addie couldn't quite hear and then asked Bernie, "You ready to go to work?"

She looked up at him, her ears pointed, alert. He smiled, nodded, and unhooked her leash. He kept the collar on, and, with her at his side, he walked over toward the area where the burn was. Then he stopped and said, "Okay, go find it."

She looked at him again uncertainly, and he knew it wasn't the right command, but, until he connected with her previous trainers, it was a little hard for him to judge. Yet she seemed to get the idea, as she turned, looked toward the burned area, and headed over, her nose down, sniffing the entire area. She wandered, while he watched, wondering if this was a complete waste of time.

When she got to the far corner and the far wall that had taken the worst of the hit, she stopped and sat down. She gave a short bark. He walked over and patted her and gave her several treats. "Good girl," he said. "Good girl."

He studied the area and realized that, short of anybody taking samples, it would be hard to know just what she had found. He sent off messages to Badger, asking if he had found any military K9 specialist there. Waiting on word from Badger, Tucker noted the flooring had space below it. He removed several of the charred floorboards, as was most of the floor. Down below was what looked like ashes. He called Rodney over.

Rodney walked up, Addie beside him, and they both took a look.

"Looks to me like you've got some questionable material down here," Tucker said. "Probably filled with gasoline or some kind of retardant and then lit on fire from this point. And it makes sense if you look at where the burn pattern is."

"Wow," Rodney said, looking from the floor underneath to the dog. "Do you think she'd recognize that scent again?"

"Well, she would," he said. "I just don't know if I can help her to understand what I need from her."

"And that's always the problem, isn't it? But the animals know and are trying to tell us." Addie smiled at Bernie. "Good girl." Bernie leaned against her leg, her tail wagging cheerfully.

"I do think they keep trying to tell us," Tucker said. "I don't think we understand them very well."

Heavy footsteps and voices approached at the front.

"And who's that?" Tucker asked, ordering Bernie back to his side. She was still an unknown quality.

"Likely the insurance adjuster and my foreman," Rodney said.

"Keep them inside, please."

"Why's that?"

"I don't want them knowing about the dog."

With that, Tucker hooked up the leash to Bernie, and, pulling Addie closer to him, he led the two of them across the floor to one of the back exits.

"Should we be leaving?" she asked quietly. "Don't you

84

think Bernie should have a chance to sniff everybody?"

"I think Rodney has an idea of who the problem is, but he doesn't quite understand how to prove it."

"Ah, so then he was hoping the dog might give him some ammunition toward that?"

"Again I haven't spoken with him, but that sounds like a likely scenario, yes."

"Right," she said, "so then we'll just have to watch and see. What if the arsonist doesn't even work here?"

"Rodney's paying a lot of people to keep them on this project, so he doesn't lose them." At that, they heard several vehicles drive up to the site.

"Wow," she said, "that's a lot of new visitors all of a sudden."

"Well, could be a shift coming on. That's possible, if they've gotten some okay to carry on in the unaffected portions," he said. "It's also fairly late in the afternoon, so I'm not sure. Maybe it's a meeting as much as anything?"

"Or another protest," she murmured.

He nodded slowly. "And that's possible too."

"Other than the loss of the pristine land out here, I never thought people would care about a building like this. Especially out here. Wouldn't it bring with it more jobs to this area?"

"And more vehicles, so more air pollution. More people, so more water pollution." Tucker shrugged. "I think it's just that everybody is upset the economy is not what it's supposed to be, and people are suffering. This is just another example of what's wrong in their world."

"It's just condos," she said.

"But, like you said earlier, it probably used to be a place where they grew up and could wander as children quite happily," he reminded her.

He walked her around the building, and she saw how far along the building project had gotten everywhere else. "So why do they start at one end and just kind of develop as they go?"

"Every builder has a different system. Sometimes with condo complexes, they take a whole unit and bring it up to the finish point, so they can rent it. Then they go complete the next unit. Other times they run through and do all the plumbing, all the wiring, and then all the interior walls, et cetera, layers after layers," he said. "It just depends on what they're comfortable with and what their time frame is."

"Okay," she said, studying it. "I don't have any experience with construction at all."

"Your father never built a house?"

"No," she said, "he's not an outdoor person at all. No, he's a doctor. So hopefully that's where his specialty is."

"Obviously, yes," he said.

She stared around. "I like this area. I wouldn't mind buying a place like this myself."

"But then where would you work?" he asked her. "It's a long commute."

"I know," she said. "I was thinking it might be time to change locations anyway, but I don't know where yet. I'm not a great one for making changes."

"Sometimes we get in a rut," he said, "and it's easier to not change. However, when we do make a change," he said, "it's often the best thing we could have done."

"I get that," she said. "I really do, but change can be scary."

"Sure it can be, and often it just makes life that much better afterward. If it's something you're afraid to do, you need to push yourself and get past that."

"*Argh*," she said, "more of those life lessons."

"I think they're great," he said with a bright smile.

She shook her head. "I don't know about that."

By the time they continued their walk, discussing the various design elements, she was surprised that they had already come all the way around.

"He does nice work," she said. "These should sell for a nice penny."

"Which is, of course, the problem," he said. "When you think about it, probably the locals themselves can't afford these."

"But they should be that much cheaper, being farther out, like he said."

"Yet, if you look at the area, it's not terribly wealthy. So likely still out of their price range."

"Hadn't considered that," she said. "And nobody likes change. Nobody likes progress. So I guess I sound just like the people around here."

"And that's where the problem comes in."

She nodded. "Interesting," she said, as she pointed out a half-dozen vehicles.

"Could be just people coming in to talk to Rodney. It could also be a new shift. It could be people trying to figure out when they're coming back to work. Maybe he called them in to discuss what they'll do about the burn area," he said with a shrug.

"Did he really offer you a job?"

"Yes," he said, "and it's something I certainly could do. The question is, is it something *I want* to do?"

"Nice to know you have so many skills," she said.

"But, like you in the ER, it doesn't mean that I necessarily *want* to utilize those skills," he murmured.

She winced. "I know. Sometimes it's easier to take a different path."

"But you can't feel guilty about that because we must do what makes us happy, not to just get through the days but to thrive," he said. "You've not had the easiest of upbringings, so you need to find something in life that makes you smile."

"And I thought that was doing the ER work," she said, "but I did find it extremely stressful. Changing that was hard, but it was the right thing to do."

CHAPTER 6

TUCKER AND ADDIE walked toward the crowd. "I suppose we should be watching Bernie's reaction?" she murmured to Tucker.

"Absolutely," he said, his voice equally quiet. "It's the dog I'll be focusing on," he said. "So let's see what Bernie comes up with."

As they walked toward the crowd, it opened slightly as Rodney stepped back to include them. He introduced them to various workers and the one insurance adjuster here.

"What kind of dog is that?" one of the guys said.

"A War Dog," Tucker said easily. And then gave a short explanation of what she'd been doing in the military. For Addie, it was interesting to see the men's reactions. Everybody was smiling and happy to see the dog. However, one guy wasn't. He caught her gaze on him and looked at her a little warily. Maybe he was scared of dogs, which was fair, because a lot of people were scared of large dogs.

Nobody questioned who she was, so she presumed they all thought that she was Tucker's partner. And that was okay with her right now. She looked over at the adjuster, busily taking notes, who seemed to be in a private conversation with Rodney. Finally the two men shook hands, and the adjuster walked away. Addie looked at Rodney, one eyebrow raised. He just smiled and nodded at her. She realized that nobody else understood what was going on either. One of the crew turned to Rodney and asked, "So when can we go back to work?"

"Waiting on the insurance," he said with a nod toward the adjuster who just left. "He'll give me a report in the next two days, and we should be back to work then."

"Right," the guy said with an eye-roll. "Like that'll happen."

"How many weeks does this set you back?" Addie asked Rodney.

"Because of where we were at in the construction process," he said, "I'll have to get new rafters brought in and new trusses, but probably," he frowned and said, "maybe two weeks."

"That's not too bad," she said, "considering that you're so much more ahead on the other units."

"Sure but we generally don't sell or have move-ins until everything's completed," he said. "So, in theory, two weeks is quite disastrous."

"But it's two weeks, not four weeks or four months," she said, reminding him.

He chuckled. "Yes, but every day in our world is about money," he said. "So it doesn't sound like a whole lot for somebody not in the industry, but it makes a huge difference in my world."

"I guess," she said. She didn't understand, but she saw the other guys were nodding with him. She thought about all the wages that went into keeping a crew on board and ready and able to work, even though they didn't put in an hour of labor, and thought that she might have a better understanding.

"Maybe we should head back now," Tucker said. He

looked down at Addie. "Are you ready to go home?"

She smiled, nodded, and tucked her hand into his, as they walked around the crowd and headed toward Tucker's truck. As they passed a couple vehicles in the parking lot where two men stood nearby, the dog stopped, and her tail went down. Bernie looked at Tucker, but he pulled on her leash, trying to move her. He stopped, looked at her, and asked, "What's the matter, girl?"

Several vehicles were parked here, and the group of people had now reformed in front of them. He looked at the two men who had been standing here. He didn't know how they were any different from the others. They were just extra crewmen to him. But not to the War Dog. He looked at Bernie and smiled, as he crouched and cuddled her gently. "Can you smell it again?"

GIVEN BERNIE'S REACTION, Tucker knew he needed to check every one of the vehicles. He said to Addie, "Let's go for a walk." Then Tucker turned to Rodney. "I'll just take Bernie over there, so she can have a look." And he headed down toward the rougher side of the property, where it wasn't paved, and then he bent to talk to Bernie. "Do you want to go to work?"

Her ears immediately lifted, and she barked. With that, he uncoupled her leash and led her through the vehicles, up to one side and down the other. She sniffed and sniffed and sniffed, and, when they got to the far end, they reached a vehicle that had been here when they arrived, parked beside two newer arrivals. As Bernie went back and forth, she finally stopped and gave a short bark at a particular vehicle and sat down. Tucker walked over and gave her treats. "Good girl," he said. "You're a very good girl."

Tucker looked over at the group, still talking among themselves, and yelled out, "Rodney, can you come here for a sec?"

Rodney nodded, made his excuses, and headed to where Tucker stood. "What's up?"

"Whose vehicle is this?" he asked.

He looked around and said, "I'm not sure. It was here this morning."

"Well, the dog has sensed something, as far as I can tell, about this vehicle."

Rodney looked at Tucker, then at the dog.

Tucker walked around the vehicle in question. The driver's side door was unlocked. Tucker pulled it open, popped the trunk, and, sure enough, inside were gas cans, gloves, matches, some other accelerants, containers, and paper. Even small pieces of wood. He looked at Rodney and said, "Well, this is your arsonist's vehicle."

He stood there, swearing gently under his breath.

"Do you know whose it is?"

He shook his head. "I don't."

As Tucker looked over, Addie opened up the passenger side and got in the glove box and pulled out the paperwork. She walked toward Tucker and Rodney. "Paperwork's here." She handed it over.

Rodney snatched it from her hand, looked at it, and said, "I don't know this name."

"And it's possible the owner has nothing to do with the arson either. The vehicle could have been stolen," Addie said.

"That could be possible too." At that, Tucker pulled out his phone and called Badger. Addie watched him and then frowned at Rodney. "Shouldn't we call the police?" she asked in a low voice.

"You mean, call them again," Rodney said, but he pulled up his phone and made some phone calls himself.

She stepped back, while the men were talking.

Tucker looked at her over his phone. He reached out a hand, she immediately placed hers in it. He whispered to her, while Badger was talking, "Are you okay?"

She nodded slowly. "I am. This is all just so weird," she murmured.

He squeezed her fingers, let her go, and returned to his call.

CHAPTER 7

ADDIE WALKED AROUND the car, noting no license plate in front or at the back of the vehicle, which gave more credence to the fact that it was likely stolen. But, at the same time, why would it have been left here? As she thought about it, it made more sense to leave it if it were stolen. The arsonist didn't want to get caught in a stolen vehicle. Plus they didn't have to take their mess with them and get caught with that either.

She stared at the mass of people still gathered here and realized that all the men were now watching them, but nobody approached. She shivered and walked closer to Tucker. He was off the phone now. As she stepped up, she said, "Are they all just watching this?"

"Yes," he said, not looking at the crowd. "Interesting, isn't it?"

"I don't understand," she said. "Wouldn't they want to be over here, asking questions about what we're doing? That would be more normal."

"Or maybe they already know," Rodney said in a hard voice. He looked at Tucker and said, "Stay here." And he turned and joined the group.

"Does he think somebody here might know something?"

"It's hard to imagine what anybody will know in this scenario," Tucker said. "This is obviously the vehicle that was used."

"And left behind because it was stolen," she said with a nod.

"It is one way to get rid of a stolen vehicle, isn't it?" he said.

"Very strange day," she said with a yawn.

He looked at her with concern. "You shouldn't have come with me," he said.

"Of course I should have," she said. "My life would be completely boring without all this."

He burst into laughter and said, "You're handling it well."

"I haven't been handling things very well in a long time," she said. "Seeing Bernie here, free and doing what she was meant to do, points it out for me."

"Hey," he said, "don't start getting depressed."

"I think it's too late for that," she said with a small laugh.

"Do you want to go home?"

"Soon," she said. "It has been a long day."

"Are you going back to your sister's?"

"Hell no," she said forcibly. "I won't contact her voluntarily for quite a while," she said. "I need time and distance from that too."

"And unfortunately," he said, "that's what your parents have been doing too."

"I know. It's the same old thing. I was trying very hard way back then," she said, "to deal with them and my sister. I don't feel like I did a very good job now."

"And that's probably how they feel. Unfortunately, once you give your power away to a person or persons," he said, "it's very hard to get it back."

"That's what I did, didn't I?" she asked in a soft voice. "I let her become the bully that she is."

"That's on her," he said in a firm voice. "What's on you is your reaction and how you handled that. You gotta stand up to bullies." Addie nodded, her expression grim. "Let me tell Rodney that we are leaving now."

Addie found the return trip just as comfortable as the initial trip and got even more familiar with him and Bernie as they made the long journey back. They stopped several times. Once just to get out and to stretch their legs, another to pick up coffee and snacks, and, when he suggested a late dinner out, she immediately agreed. Anything to keep this relationship ongoing.

She didn't know what would happen when they got back to Miami, but she didn't want to lose track of Tucker. Maybe that was just selfish of her, but she also didn't want to lose track of Bernie. The thought that the dog had the same name as her sister was now an irritant more than anything because, every time she saw the dog, she was thinking of her sister and her horrible behavior. "Do you think my sister is still a threat to Bernie?"

"I would hope not," he said, "but your sister's an unknown quality. I don't know how far she'll go to get her way."

At that, Addie frowned. "Well, I hope not this far, because, well"—she shook her head—"I just don't know. I just don't want any more of this. I want it to be done now."

"So maybe she'll have learned something about this scenario and will want it over too."

"I hope so," she said. "Are you looking forward to the wedding now?"

"Well, I'm better prepared for the wedding since saving

the dog, visiting the fire site, and finding the vehicle used in the arson," he said. "The rehearsal's tomorrow—Friday afternoon—with the dinner that night," he added. "I always think of it as being the wedding, but it isn't. Obviously the wedding's on Saturday."

"How big is the wedding?"

"They told me that it wouldn't be very big, so I don't know," he said. "I haven't been very good about asking for any details."

She nodded. "Of course not, if you've been trying to avoid the whole thing."

"And that's probably wrong of me too," he admitted. "Sometimes there are just more to family needs than you expect."

"Particularly if you came close to dying," she reminded him.

He nodded. "And I do tend to forget that. Because I lived it and survived, I figure everybody else lived and survived it too and have moved on. But my sister still gets pretty emotional about it."

"Also she and Rodney have had a long time to get to this point," she added, "and she's waited until you were back on your feet. So it matters to her to have you there."

"Do you think they didn't get married all this time because I wasn't on my feet?" he asked, turning to frown at her.

"It would make sense to me. If it was just the two of us, I would want my brother there too."

"I didn't even consider that," he confessed. "That makes me feel even shittier."

She laughed. "You'll make up for it by being there," she said with a bright smile.

He nodded. "And if I can help my brother-in-law, then

I'll do that."

"And you already talk to him as if he's your brother-in-law, which I find interesting."

"Well, he's been in the family for a long time now," he murmured. "I can't see that the wedding certificate will make any difference."

"I like that," she said. "It's nice to think that he's already so accepted that the adjustments have already been done."

"Well, I imagine there are plenty more adjustments to expect because I did hear from various people that having that wedding certificate does make a difference, although I don't quite understand how or why."

"I imagine it makes some difference, just like everything in life does. There's a sense of reverence about making a commitment like that. Or at least I feel like there should be."

"Agreed." Tucker pulled into the restaurant's parking lot and escorted Addie to the entrance.

The hostess greeted them and directed them to a table.

"Have you ever been here before?" she asked, looking around.

He shook his head. "No, I haven't," he said. "The food looks good though." He tapped the menu.

"And I'm hungry," she said. "Lately I haven't been eating much."

"Too much upset going on in your world," he said.

"I guess," she said. As they sat here, waiting for their order to come, they carried on with the same easygoing conversation that they'd started. Finally she pointed it out. "You do realize how well we're getting along and how easy it is to talk to you, huh?"

"I was just thinking that," he said. "It doesn't always happen, does it?"

"No, but when people click, they click," she said with a smile.

He nodded. "Nice to see that too," he said. "I felt like I was a fish out of water for the longest time. When you've been in a major accident, you know that a lot of other people don't even know how to relate. They don't have a clue on what to do or what to say, so they ignore it all, which, in a way, is best," he said, "or they awkwardly compensate by making it out that you're incapable of doing anything."

She burst out laughing. "Oh, isn't that funny how, when you've got a broken leg, sometimes people speak louder because it's as if you're suddenly deaf too."

"And it's so darn frustrating," he said with a grin. "At this point, I've just learned to smile and to accept it and to ignore it all."

"It's really all you can do," she said. "We nurses see that all the time. People just don't have any experience dealing with something like that, so they don't know how to react."

He grinned at her. "And that's very true," he said, "but that's also what makes you very different. You have experiences that I can relate to."

"And you have experiences I can relate to," she said with a nod. "I think all of that helps make it feel like I already know so much about you."

As they sat here, going back and forth, mentioning bits and pieces of their lives, places more relatable in blocks of time, she said, "I wish we didn't have to leave Bernie in the truck."

He nodded. "And speaking of that," he said, "I think I'll go check on her." She frowned, and he shook his head. "I'll be back in five minutes," he said. "By then we should be served."

"Okay," she said, and she watched nervously as he headed to the truck. She didn't know why she was nervous, but just the thought of being separated from Bernie and Tucker gave Addie anxiety. And that was just stupid. She'd been an independent female for a long time. She should be sitting here and smiling to herself because she finally met somebody who she really liked.

Instead she was almost getting depressed at the thought of being separated in a couple hours from his presence, and they hadn't even been together very long. But the time they had been together had been incredibly powerful, she admitted. So what would she do about it now? How strange this whole mess was. Still, she sat here and waited, and, when their meals arrived, she realized how long Tucker had been gone. She pulled out her phone and quickly sent him a text. **Meals are here.**

When there was no answer, she froze, then quickly dialed him, but he didn't answer his phone either. When the waitress came back, Addie said, "I'm sorry. There's been an emergency. Can we pack the meals to go, please?" The waitress stared at her a second, but looked down at the burgers and fries, then nodded. She took the plates away, and, by the time she returned, Addie was standing up and had already put the money on the table for their bill. The waitress handed her the take-out bags. Addie thanked her and raced out the door.

Once outside, she stopped. The truck was still there—thank God—but she saw no sign of either Bernie or Tucker. Maybe he'd taken her out so she could go to the …

At the truck, she put the food items in the front seat, noting that it was unlocked, but then he would have unlocked the door in order to get the dog out, and then she raced around, looking for him. When she found no sign in the parking lot, she started calling out. She called his phone again, and, when it rang at the edge of the parking lot, alongside the woods, she raced over, following the sound, until she caught a glimpse of something in the long grass. His phone. Her heart sank.

She snatched his phone, swiped it like she'd seen him do, and called the last number. With the words tumbling over each other, she tried to tell the guy that Tucker had gone missing.

Badger calmly said, "Let's take this from the top. How long has he been missing?"

She took a long slow deep breath. "I can't really say. Maybe fifteen minutes. I found his phone in the brush."

"And that's, of course, the most worrying part," he said. "Stay very calm, and stay at that location. We'll use satellite to track you."

She didn't even think about that. Maybe that's just what these people did. As soon as he came back online, he said, "Somebody is coming toward you."

"A cop?" She looked around nervously.

"Actually it'll be Tucker's brother-in-law."

"Rodney? Was he still at the site?"

"We caught him on his way back too," he said. "So he should be pulling into the restaurant any minute."

"Oh, thank you," she said. "I just can't imagine what happened."

"I imagine either he was kidnapped or attacked," Badger said without mincing his words. "But I don't want you searching the woods there on your own, in case the attacker is still there."

"You could have said something else," she said in exasperation, "something that wouldn't send me into a panic."

"Maybe, but it wouldn't have been the truth," he said, "and I'm on the side of life that deals with the truth."

Just then she heard a voice calling out to her.

"Addie, you here?"

She turned and saw Rodney and ran to him. "My God," she said, "I don't know what happened." He quickly asked for a breakdown. She gave it to him. He nodded and said, "That's what Badger said to me."

She held up the phone. "I have Badger on the phone right now." She put it on Speaker, and Badger spoke up.

"Rodney, take a good look around the woods there. See if Tucker's lying unconscious somewhere."

"I'm on it," Rodney said, his voice grim. He turned to look at Addie. "You stay here."

"Hell no," she said. "Two sets of eyes are better than one."

"It's almost dark," he said. "Nobody can see anything."

"All the more reason," she said, "for both of us to look. We don't have any time."

He snorted. "At least this way I won't have to worry about you disappearing too."

"What if another vehicle came and got him?" she asked both Rodney and Badger.

"We're looking at the video cameras right now," Badger said, his voice calm. "The only way that would have happened is if he were attacked and knocked unconscious. Did you hear or see anything when you were in the restaurant?"

"No, he only went back to check on the dog."

"Of course he did."

"But why would somebody be following him?" she murmured.

"Which could indicate this mess is linked to the fire scenario," Badger said.

Rodney stopped, looked at the phone, and said, "That's exactly what's happened, isn't it? Whoever was involved in the arson case was likely part of the crowd there."

"Give me the names of whoever was there," Badger said.

Rodney immediately reeled off names. "They all work for me, either on a full-time or a contract basis," he said.

"And give us the date of the fire and the time of the fire," Badger said, "so we can check out alibis."

"Well, I can give you the basics," he said, "and you can talk to a Detective Watson at the local precinct, who has it under investigation."

"Will do." At that, Badger said, "I'll ring off. Let me know as soon as you find out anything."

"Well, I hope I find out something fast," she said, "because any other answer will be bad news."

"Don't even go there," Badger said. "Tucker is an old hand at this."

"Says you," she said, "but nobody gets lucky every time."

"Which is why he had his accident. We've already told him that he's used up a couple of his lives, and he needs to be more careful," he said with a note of humor.

"That's not funny," she said. "I don't want anything to happen to him."

"Good," he said in the gentlest of voices, "and that thought alone will help him fight a little more."

With that, Badger hung up, leaving her staring at the phone, wondering exactly what he meant. But Rodney raced ahead in the woods.

"If you go too fast," she said, trying to keep up, "we won't see him." She turned Tucker's phone to Flashlight mode and used it to peer through the area. She looked down and grabbed Rodney's arm. "There are tracks through here," she said, pointing out a spot where the weeds had parted under heavy traffic. Rodney looked at it, nodded, and the two of them raced in that direction. "Do you think it's safe?"

"Safe for us or safe for him?"

"Should we call out for him?"

He hesitated and then shook his head. "I don't think it matters at this point. We need to find him." He raised his voice and yelled out, "Tucker! Where are you, Tucker? Answer me."

With him calling, she raised her voice at the same time, and the two of them went slightly different directions, calling out for Tucker. They kept at it for a good ten to fifteen minutes, and then they both stopped and looked at each other. She strained her ears and called out once as loud as she could. "Tucker!" Then she thought more about it and called out, "Bernie, bark!" She yelled again, "Bernie, bark!"

Up the path came a small *yelp*. They looked at each other and tore in the direction of the bark from the dark.

TUCKER OPENED HIS eyes, stifling the groan seeping through his taut lips. Tucker knew from old times that, upon first waking up, the silence was instinctive, now ingrained only after long years of training and experience. He'd taken a blow to the head. A blow he hadn't seen coming. He was on the forest floor and reached out a hand, and it landed on a furry back. Hearing a whine from the animal, he opened his eyes. Bernie sat here, looking down at him, worry in her huge chocolate-colored eyes. She leaned over and nudged his cheek and chin with her nose. He reached up and gently stroked her.

"Hey, girl," he whispered. "You're standing guard over me." She gave a tiny whine again and then laid down alongside him, her body heat soaking into his. He lay here for a long moment, regaining his breath and a sense of awareness as to where he was and what had happened. He reached up a hand to the sore spot on his head, and his fingers came away sticky. Almost no daylight remained, and it was hard to see anything.

In the distance, he heard the brush being trashed as somebody raced through the trees. It didn't take much longer to realize the sounds were coming toward him. He put a hand on the dog's neck and, using her for support, pulled himself up to a sitting position. He didn't know if it was a friend or foe racing toward him, but he needed to be prepared if it were the latter. He heard somebody call out, and then the dog barked again. He calmed her down and whispered, "Stay quiet, stay quiet." Then he heard a female calling out, "Tucker!"

With his croaking voice, he answered, "I'm here."

Seconds later two people broke into the clearing where he sat and came to a dead stop. Shock, relief, and dismay were on their faces. Addie raced over and dropped to her knees beside him. "Oh, my God," she said. "Are you okay?"

"I'm not sure yet," he said. "I just woke up a few moments ago."

"You've been missing for hours," she whispered, her hand going to his head. He winced as she touched the wound, but, remembering she was a nurse, he let her take a look at it. She had a phone in her hand, turned on the flashlight, and took a good look. "You'll need stitches," she announced. "Let me see if there's any other damage."

He lay back down again, as she did a quick check of his body. Everything felt okay, but he couldn't be sure because he hadn't stood yet. She checked his eyes, noted that his pupils were at least moving properly. "Somebody attacked you from behind, I presume, given the site of the injury," she said quietly, as she sat back on her knees.

He looked at her, frowned, and said, "The last thing I remember was going to the truck to let Bernie here out."

"You said you would check on her, and you left me inside the restaurant."

"I didn't even hear anything around me. Next thing I knew, something smashed into the back of my head, and I woke up here."

"Why would they drag you out here and leave you?" she murmured.

"It's hard to say," Rodney said, behind her. "Maybe he thought that Tucker was alone and didn't know you were here too."

"And yet, if we're working on the theory that the arsonist followed us here, then he would know that I left the arson site with Tucker," she said, looking back at Rodney.

"Maybe they thought he'd dropped you off already."

"I don't know, Rodney. That's kind of flimsy," she murmured. "Or whoever it was thought I would take off because Tucker stood me up?" She shrugged. "Whatever the reason, you're big and heavy when conscious. So you're a dead weight to carry," she said. "And you're out here, some distance from the restaurant."

"But am I still on the property?" he asked, as he sat back up again.

"I don't know about on the property," Rodney said,

"but you're not that far away."

"So somebody big enough to carry me," Tucker said. "The question is, why?"

"Unless they thought the blow to your head was more than they had expected it to be," she said, "and then figured that, if they'd killed you, they might want your body far enough away that nobody would find you for a while," she said.

"That would imply that they panicked," he said, reaching up and holding his head. He suddenly lunged to his feet, where he stood with his legs spread apart as he braced himself to stop the swaying. Addie wrapped her arm around him. "Use me to help stabilize yourself," she urged.

He slung his arm around her shoulders and let her take some of his weight.

"What about Bernie?" she asked. "What would they have done with her?"

"I presume they weren't armed," Rodney said. "Otherwise there was no point in keeping you alive."

"Meaning?" Addie asked.

"Well, they could have shot Tucker and the dog."

"Hadn't thought of that," Tucker said. "So we'll assume they didn't have a gun, or they didn't dare take a chance of anybody hearing the shot," he said.

"Where was the dog when all this was happening? What would she have done?" Addie murmured.

"I opened the truck door. She jumped down. After that, I don't know what happened. She doesn't know me that well, and she is a little confused still with her transition to civilian life."

"I'd assume she'd have run away far enough to get out of the guy's reach, just in case he was trying to grab her too,"

Addie murmured out loud.

"Well, I sure as hell wouldn't want anybody grabbing me," Tucker said. "I'm not sure about what she would have done though."

"I think she stayed at a distance, and, when they dropped you, she stayed around to make sure that you were okay. Once the guy left, she came in close to keep you company, until you woke up," she murmured. "That's typical dog behavior."

"I'm not sure that's even what happened," he said. "We're just doing best guesses at the moment."

"It's all we have," she said. "How we'll find out beyond that, I don't know." She looked at Rodney. "Lead the way back to the truck," she said.

He nodded, fell into step just ahead of them, and she urged Tucker to move forward behind Rodney. "I'm coming," he said. "The head's just pounding pretty good."

"Let's get you back to the truck," she said, "and I'll drive you to the hospital, so we can get that head wound stitched up."

"I'm okay without the stitches."

"No, you're not," she said, arguing fiercely. "I get that you're a big tough guy, but I'm also the nurse. That wound needs to be closed."

Tucker groaned. "That just means questions and all kinds of BS that I don't have time for."

"You'll make time," she said. "So we either do it the easy way or the hard way."

He looked down at her in amusement. "And you'll stop me, one way or the other?"

"Hell yes," she said, "and, if that doesn't work, I'll enlist your sister."

Immediately Rodney burst out laughing. "I like her," he said.

Tucker groaned. "She certainly knows how to wield a weapon."

"You know perfectly well your sister won't let you get away with not getting this checked out," she said, "so it's a good weapon to pick."

"I know," he said. "Fine, we'll go to the hospital, but only if it'll be fast. I have absolutely no intention of sitting there for three hours before they even take a look at me."

"If it's that bad," she said, "I can get the materials and stitch it up myself."

"Well then, let's just do that."

"No," she said. "Hospital first."

He sighed. "They'll just take x-rays, tell me that I got a concussion, and send me home for the next few days."

"Is there anything wrong with that?" she asked.

"I already know it, so why go?"

"Stop being a child," she scolded.

He didn't know how to get her to stop talking, but she was making his headache worse. "Don't yell. You're making my head pound," he said. "I already have a bad enough headache."

She groaned. "Fine, as long as you agree to go to the hospital."

"I said I would," he said.

"I just don't want an argument when we get you to the truck."

Up ahead he saw the parking lot. "Looks like the truck's right there." He turned to Rodney and said, "You could drive."

"Oh no," he said. "I know what you'll do. You'll try to

TUCKER

convince me to not take you to the hospital. I saw the cut myself. I think it needs stitches."

Tucker sighed. "You're both against me," he snapped.

"If looking after you means being against you, then we're both against you," she said immediately. "And, once again, you're acting like a two-year-old."

Rodney burst out laughing again. "She's definitely got your number."

"That's not fair," Tucker said. By the time he made it to the truck, he could feel the sweat pouring off him. He knew he'd been a little more injured than he'd expected and hoped. He'd always had an ability to bounce back, but, since his accident, that ability seemed to have been taken from him. Whenever he caught a cold or there was a flu around, he succumbed way too easily. He figured that this would be the same deal. He walked around to the side of the truck and then stopped because she was slipped under his arm and now leaning against the driver's door.

"What are you doing?" he asked in confusion.

"You're not driving," she said. "I will."

He looked at her, then at Rodney, who just nodded.

Tucker sighed louder this time. "Fine," he said. "We need to get the dog in though."

"She'll come up without a problem," she said calmly. She looked at Bernie. "Won't you, girl?"

Bernie barked at her in delight. Addie opened up the back seat and helped the dog into the back.

"She won't stay back there," he said.

"That's fine. I just need to get you around to your side," she said, eyeing him steadily. Trying to make it look like it was easier than it was, he made his way around to the passenger side and slowly crawled in. Immediately the smell of food wafted toward him. He looked at the bags beside him. "What's this?"

"Our dinner," she said with a wry look. "You never came back to the restaurant, so I came out. I had them pack it up to-go, before I came looking for you. I found your phone at the corner of the parking lot, which is when I phoned Badger." He stared at her. She shrugged. "He contacted Rodney, and Rodney was already on his way from the site, so he stopped and helped me to find you."

"Wow," he said. "Well, I guess it all ends well and much better than it could have."

"Absolutely. For all I know, us calling for you sent this guy running away," she said. "Maybe he would have stayed and taken care of you forever," she murmured. "I don't know what's going on. But let's get you to the hospital and get one thing taken care of." She looked at Rodney and asked, "Are you coming to the hospital?"

He shook his head. "Keep in touch though," he said. "I've got to go home to my soon-to-be wife." And, with that, he lifted a hand and headed to his truck.

"I'll update Badger," Addie said.

Tucker didn't argue.

CHAPTER 8

ADDIE PULLED OUT of the restaurant parking lot, wondering at the strange turn of events. Instead of a nice dinner—almost a date scenario—she was now taking Tucker to the hospital. But the hospital wasn't very far away, and she knew the area well. When she neared the emergency entrance, she parked in the temporary parking lot. She got out and helped him inside. Several of the staff recognized her, and she was lucky enough that they checked out Tucker's head and immediately moved him into a room.

She went back outside, checked on Bernie, parked the truck in the main parking area out of the way, and came back in again. As she entered his hospital room, the doctor stood over Tucker, studying his head wound.

"How bad is it?" she asked. When the doctor turned, she recognized him. "Hey, Jim. How you doing?"

"Hey, Addie. How are you?"

"Well, I wasn't doing too bad," she said, "until this guy got injured." She walked over to stand beside the patient. Tucker reached up a hand; she immediately grabbed it and held it tight. "How bad is the head?"

"Well, the wound's pretty deep," Jim said. "We'll get in quite a few stitches here, and he's got a concussion. He'll be sore for the next couple days." He looked down at Tucker and said, "I'll freeze this, so I can get the stitches in. You got a problem with that?"

Tucker just gave him a hard look. "Not at all."

She stood at his side, while a nurse came in and cleaned the wound, and then the doctor returned to stitch it up. Jim looked Tucker over as he talked, all the while sewing. "Any other wounds?"

"Not that we saw," she said quietly.

"Did you call the police?"

"Not yet, but it's likely related to a case that they're already working on," Tucker said.

The doctor shook his head. "It's a sad world these days," he said, but he finished quickly and looked down at her and asked, "Will you look after him?"

"Absolutely," she said.

"Well then, you know the routine," he said. "I'll write a prescription for some painkillers, but, other than that, get him to a doctor in a few days or so—or earlier if there are any problems."

"Will do," she said with a bright smile. She watched and waited, and it took another thirty minutes before Jim returned, and she had a prescription in her hand. Thanking him again, Jim left. She looked over at Tucker, who was lying on the bed with his eyes closed. "Why don't you stay here overnight?" she asked impulsively.

His eyes flew open, and he stared out of these bright blue eyes, strong, determined, immediately rejecting her suggestion.

She smiled and said, "Okay. You can't blame me for at least trying."

"I don't do well in hospitals," he said.

And then she thought about all the injuries he'd been through and the number of times he must have been in hospitals. She realized that emotionally this was not where he needed to be. She nodded. "Then, if you're ready," she said, "let's get you home."

"I don't even know where home is at the moment," he said, "but I do have a hotel room."

She hesitated and then said, "I don't want you to be alone tonight."

"It's just a head injury," he said dismissively.

She snorted. "Just a head injury?" she asked. "I'm pretty sure *just a head injury* means a whole lot more than what you're thinking."

"Maybe," he said, as he slowly sat up, reaching for the bars alongside the upper half of the bed for balance.

She stepped in front of him and asked, "How about a wheelchair?"

He snorted at that.

She shrugged. "Had to try."

"This is where I clearly see that you're a nurse," he said with a small grin.

"Yep," she said, "and looking after patients is what I do. And I'm used to difficult patients."

"If you can get me back to the hotel," he said, "I promise I'll be fine in the morning."

She frowned at that, but he wasn't giving her any choice. She helped him back out to the truck, and, once they were settled inside, with Bernie sitting in the front between them again, she asked, "Are you allowed to bring a dog in the hotel?"

He looked down, groaned, and said, "No. I thought I'd sneak her in."

Addie turned on the engine and headed to the main road. When they pulled up and stopped, he opened his eyes and said, "This is not my hotel."

"That's because it's my place," she said. "Come on. I've got a spare room, and I don't have a problem keeping Bernie as well."

He looked at her for a long moment and then shrugged and said, "Thank you. It's decent of you to offer."

"I won't leave an injured man alone with a dog that needs a whole lot more than an injured man for reassurance in a hotel," she said. "The dog needs more than that, even if you think you don't."

"I'm used to being alone," he said quietly.

"I get it. But maybe you need to get used to not being alone so much."

She opened up the truck door, hopped out, and let Bernie out. Then she walked the dog to Tucker's door in time to help him as he slid from the passenger side. She looked at him, shook her head, and said, "You're not looking so good."

She reached past him and picked up their dinners from the footwell. Then she walked with him carefully up the concrete path toward her front door. "I have a fenced backyard," she said, calling Bernie to her. The dog came racing, sniffed the bags, and then stayed at her side the whole time. "And where's the dog food?" she asked Tucker.

"It's still in the back of the truck," he said.

"I'll get it later," she said.

"It's probably too heavy for you," he said. "I didn't think about you dealing with it. I just bought a big bag."

"Not a problem," she said. "I'll figure it out." She unlocked her place and pushed open the door and let him in. A big recliner was off to the side. She pointed it out and said, "Why don't you just sit down and relax?"

He looked at it and gratefully eased himself into the seat.

"This is a big chair," he said, settling in.

"Yes," she said. "I like them that way."

"Good choice," he said, stretching out with his eyes closed again.

"Do you want any food?" she asked, closing the front door and walking through to the kitchen on the same pathway. She opened up the back door and let Bernie out. Addie propped open the door and said, "It's also nice outside, if you want to sit out there."

He made his way from the big recliner and out to the backyard. He sat on the deck at the tiny patio table and smiled. "It's small, but it suits you."

"It was a place to get away," she said. "It came on the market pretty cheap, during one of the many economic depressions, and I bought it," she said. "I haven't regretted it."

"There's nothing like having your own space," he said.

"Do you want anything to eat or drink yet?"

"No," he said. "I was looking at buying a place in this next year or so, but I had my accident first, and now I'm not sure where and what I'm doing."

"Right," she said, "you better phone Rodney and let him know that you're okay."

"I already did," he said.

"Okay, I'll go out and see if I can lift that bag of dog food."

"Alternatively," he said, "because I know it's heavy, maybe just take a bowl out, open up a corner, and bring in some dog food for her."

"That works too," she said. She probably wasn't capable of getting the bag out on her own, and she didn't want him even trying. But, if he saw her struggling, then chances were he would try to get it out for her. She went in and grabbed a big mixing bowl and headed out to the truck, feeling a little foolish. She cut open the top of the bag dipped the bowl inside until it was full, grabbed the pack of treats, and brought them back into the house too.

As soon as Bernie saw her, she came running, trying to get into the bowl. Addie walked into the kitchen, laughing, and divvied it into a smaller bowl and took it outside on the deck. She filled a matching bowl full of water and put it down for the dog too. Bernie immediately dove into the bowl of food.

"Now that's what I like to see," she said, "a healthy appetite."

"Well, I had an appetite," he said, "but that was before getting my head smashed."

"And we do have our dinner all boxed up," she said, "if you want to try that."

"We might as well warm it up," he said. "Maybe I'll get a little down."

"I have an air fryer. I can toss in all the fries and see if I can crisp them back up again."

"You do that," he said. "I'll just sit here and rest."

She went through the motions of rewarming the meat out of the buns, remade the burgers, and put the fries into the air fryer. By the time it was all ready and hot at the same time, she carried it out to find him gently sleeping beside her. She set down the plates quietly.

"I'm not sleeping."

"Too bad," she said. "I wish you were."

"I'm fine," he said, opening his eyes and smiling at her.

"You're a tough nut."

"And I have a tough head, yes," he said with a slight

nod. "And a strong constitution, which was a good thing when I was on missions," he said, "because I do heal fast."

"Well, you used to," she said, "but every time it's different. And the more injuries you have, the slower you heal."

"And I probably used up all my goodwill in healing by now," he said, "but I don't feel that bad."

"Good painkillers," she said cheerfully. She nudged his plate and said, "See if you can get some food down."

He took one look, smiled, and said, "This looks good. Location-wise, your place is much nicer than the restaurant."

"Just a few hours later eating our dinner," she said. "We didn't expect that jaunt to the hospital."

"No, but all's well that ends well."

TUCKER FINISHED THE burger and looked at his empty plate. "Considering that was warmed up from a couple hours ago," he said, "it tasted surprisingly well."

"Good," she said, "also good on that maybe you're not feeling too bad."

"Nothing a good night's sleep won't fix," he said. He looked down to see Bernie lying at his feet with a hopeful look in her eyes. He smiled and said, "I don't have anything for you, girl."

She just laid her head on his foot, and he reached down and scratched her gently.

"What's the chance of you getting some hands-on training for her?" she asked him curiously.

He looked up at her. "What are you thinking?"

"There's probably a need for her services," she said. "When you consider it, she could do an awful lot to help people. It would be a hell of a new job for you too."

"Instead of construction?" he asked with a smile.

"I get the idea that the construction job is a temporary one for you, but maybe I'm wrong." She shrugged. "It's your life. I don't mean to be getting too involved."

"You can be involved all you want," he said, "but I don't know what I want to do. I think it's a good idea, and I have put out a couple queries into such a training program," he said, as he gently patted the dog on the head. "I think she would enjoy it."

"She would enjoy a lot of things," she said. "Hikes in the mountains and walks in the woods and even running along a beach. An outdoor lifestyle for the dog would be great, but it's a matter of what can you and she do to earn a living? And what do you want to do for yourself? If you don't want to work with the dog full-time, then that's not the avenue to go. Maybe you could take her to the job on the construction sites."

"That's possible too," he said, as he shrugged. Just then his phone rang. He looked down and smiled. "It's my sister." He hit the Talk button and left it on Speakerphone. "I'm fine, sis."

"Are you sure?" she asked, almost wailing. "Rodney told me all about it."

"Well," he said, "I'm fine. I'm sitting at Addie's place. We just had our restaurant meals warmed up. I've got stitches in my head, and I'll be fine after a good night's sleep."

"How come you keep getting injured?" she asked, still in a teary voice. "I can't stand to see you hurting all the time."

"Well, this time, I'm not sure, but I think it was connected to Rodney's construction site."

"He did imply something along that line," she said, sniffling. "I just think that's terrible."

"Personally I'm not feeling all that great about it either."

She gave a long noisy sigh. "Do I need to push off the wedding?"

"Good Lord, no," he said. "You and he have pushed that off long enough."

"I want you there," she murmured.

"And I'll be there," he said. "Don't worry. I do have to get down there though. Why you chose Saint Pete's and Tampa, I don't know."

"Because that's where so many of my friends are," she said. "It seemed easier to make us go there than to have everybody inconvenienced to come here."

He shook his head. "Honestly," he said, "you should be doing whatever you want to do, and don't worry about them."

"I just want to get married," she said. "It's taken me a long time to get to this point, and, now that you're here, I want to make sure I get the job done."

"Then I'll be there," he said, and, just as they went to hang up, he asked, "By the way, can I bring a friend?"

"Addie, you mean?"

"Yes," he said, turning to look at Addie, whose eyebrows shot up. "If you don't mind."

"No, not at all," she said. "I'd love to meet her. Rodney says she was great."

"If that means that she insisted I go to the hospital and get stitches in my head, then yes," he said in a dry tone.

"Anybody who can handle you gets a thumbs-up from me. But the fact that she got you to a hospital for treatment is two thumbs-up."

And, with that, and bright laughter, she hung up. He looked at Addie, who stared at him. "Sorry. I kind of sprung that on you," he said. "Don't feel like you have to say yes, but I just wanted to make that invitation possible."

"Absolutely," she said. "And it would be fun."

"Good," he said, "it would be nice to have somebody there too."

"Ah, that silent-support thing."

"Yes," he said. "It's kind of odd, when you think about it. But, after going to so many weddings, it seems like I end up as the odd man out. Hate that."

"At the same time, I understand completely. Is it a formal affair though?" she asked, worried.

He said, "I'm wearing a suit, not a tux."

"Ah," she said and turned to look back at her house. "I just don't know if I have anything to wear."

"I can tell you quite honestly that my sister couldn't care less. She's been working toward this wedding for a long time, but she's the one who's been holding back. So I don't think having the right clothes to wear is a problem for her. Believe me. I do understand the need to at least be within the range of a proper dress code."

"Yes," she said, "but it'll be in Saint Pete's Beach, right?" Tucker nodded. "So maybe just a sundress will do."

"We have a long drive too," he said. "I've got a hotel room there for the night. If you want, you can share it with me."

She looked at him in surprise and then said, "You know what? That might be quite nice."

"Good," he said. "It's a deal. I'll stay here tonight, and you can come to the wedding with me and stay there with me over the weekend."

"I don't think I've ever been to Saint Pete's Beach."

"Miles of white sand, dotted by various benches touting ads with hotel-themed colors all up and down the beach," he said. "Very much a tourist trap but, if you step out of that to just enjoy Mother Nature, what she has to offer is beautiful."

"Great," she said. "I'm looking forward to that. In the meantime," she said, standing up and pulling the plates toward her, "I'll clean up the kitchen. It is quite late, and I'm getting tired. So I'll have a shower, and I'll show you to your room."

"And what about Bernie here?" he asked. Bernie just looked exhausted at his feet.

"I figured we'd give her the inside of the house. What do you think? Take her out one more time before bed, then tuck her in for the night with us."

"I think that's a good idea. If we leave the bedroom doors open, she'll come and go, as she needs to make sure that we're still here. She'll likely have abandonment issues for quite a while."

"I can't imagine how she wouldn't," she said. "I feel like I'll have abandonment issues if you take her away. She was always really close with me, but I'm just not set up for a big dog like that," she said, motioning around at the small house. "No doggie doors. Long hours at work. Floating days on and off."

"It doesn't seem like a long-term solution for you here."

"It isn't," she said. "It was a solution to get away from my family."

"Speaking of which," he said, "have you had any contact with your sister?"

She pulled up her phone, checked, and said, "There's a text from her, asking where I am."

"You didn't answer her?"

"I didn't see it until now," she said with a shrug. "I've been a little busy."

"Understood," he said, "looking after me. Sorry about that."

She looked up, smiled, and said, "I'd rather look after you than her."

"Well, I'd rather you didn't have to look after either of us," he said. "Not exactly the strong macho male I'd like to appear as."

She snorted. "Nothing personal," she said, "but that's very overrated."

He burst out laughing. "Well, I'm glad you think so," he said, "because really, at this point, it's all about making the best of the situation."

"I guess the question is, do you think we were followed here, like they followed us to the restaurant from the construction site?" she asked. "It occurred to me when I was driving, but I didn't want to bring it up because you were dozing."

"I was thinking about it too, and I've texted Badger about that. Texted Rodney as well."

"I have a security system," she said. "It's not much, but it is something."

"Well, let's get it set," he said, standing up to his feet. "First I'll take the dog out and give her a chance to go to the bathroom. Then I'll bring her in, and we'll go upstairs."

She nodded and headed into the kitchen. He walked around the backyard and waited for Bernie to do her business and then headed back inside, asking Addie for a bag. She shrugged and said, "I don't really have any poop bags, but here's a kitchen bag." So she gave him a small bag.

He cleaned up the mess and put it in the garbage can outside, his gaze assessing, as he looked around the area to ensure nothing new or different was going on, hating the thickness in his head. Just one of the reasons why he didn't like taking medications; they always dulled his senses. If they were still in danger, he didn't want to consider being attacked while drugged.

With the kitchen done and the dog happy to come inside, they set the security system and headed upstairs. He was pleased to see that his body moved easier, and climbing the stairs didn't make him dizzy or light-headed. She showed him the spare room, and he nodded in approval. "Nice and simple. Thank you."

"And your bathroom's here," she said. "I have an en suite in my room." She led the way into the master, and she gave him a quick tour of her place. "I'll sleep here."

"Leave the door open for the dog," he said.

"Sure." She smiled and said, "Good night then."

He cleared his throat. She stopped, looked at him in a questioning manner, and he said, "I did want to thank you for looking after me today."

She gave him a beaming smile. "It was a pleasure," she said. "It's not exactly the trip that I had imagined, but, hey, it was a whole lot better than sitting at home, wondering how I was related to my sister," she admitted. "Now go get some sleep."

"Will do." He gave her a boyish grin and asked, "Don't I get a kiss good night?"

She shook her head. Tucker now flashed that wicked grin of his at her, and she said, "Well, considering you're injured, it's probably safe tonight." She reached up and kissed him ever-so-gently on the cheek. "Now go to bed," she said firmly, and she stepped inside her room and pushed the door slightly closed but didn't shut it fully.

He looked down at Bernie. "I guess that's us being told, huh?"

Bernie barked once, and Tucker led the way back to the bedroom, where he stretched out fully on the bed. With a nice happy sigh, Bernie laid down on the fluffy rug beside his bed. He smiled and said, "Have a good night, sweetie. Your life's changed for the better."

And he closed his eyes. He didn't even attempt to get changed or undress. Although he knew that some of his clothing had blood on it, most of it had dried, and he didn't even have a change of clothes anyway. He would return to the hotel, gather his things, and check out.

Soon enough they would be on their way to a Saint Pete's hotel for the rehearsal. He knew that his sister was likely to let him off the hook for the rehearsal because of his injury. But was it fair to do that? On the other hand, why did he need to rehearse walking Molly down the aisle? Rodney would certainly give Tucker a pass, especially understanding that Tucker's injury was probably involved with Rodney's arson case. The bride and groom had enough problems right now without things going any crazier in the wrong direction. It was a matter of making the wedding weekend happen in a commonsense way.

He closed his eyes, only to have them open a few seconds later. But, when he checked his watch, he noted it was now two o'clock in the morning, and he'd been asleep for hours.

He frowned, looked down at the dog. She was lying there with her eyes open, her ears alert. "Yeah, you hear it too, don't you? But what are we hearing?"

He slowly stood and walked to the window. His room faced the street, and he couldn't see anything. Of course, at that hour of the morning, what was he expecting? He moved down the stairs with the dog carefully at his side and walked around the lower portion of the house, wondering what he had heard. As he got to the back door, she whined. He opened the door and let her out. She immediately bounded into the backyard, growling. As soon as she growled, he stepped behind cover, trying to see what she saw. Nobody was in the backyard, but that didn't mean that someone hadn't been there a few moments ago. She sniffed and walked around with her head down. "What are you smelling, little one?"

In the distance, he heard trees rustle and footsteps, but the sounds were now faint. "You chase somebody away, did you?"

But was it in this backyard, or was it in somebody else's?

All the yards were fairly small and piled in on top of each other, so he couldn't be sure which yard the person had been in. Considering their intruder took off rapidly, Tucker was pretty damn sure whoever it was, was up to no good. When Bernie returned, he sat outside with her for a good ten minutes, but it was calm and quiet. Finally he stood, walked back inside with Bernie, reset the alarms, and said, "Come on, girl. Let's go get some more sleep."

As he went upstairs, he saw Addie standing at the landing, her robe clutched around her chest and neck, as she stared at him. "What did you hear?" she asked him.

"I'm not sure, but Bernie didn't growl until we got outside. If somebody was there, Bernie chased them away. I can't be sure the intruder was in your yard, as they are all so close."

She nodded slowly. "I heard you go downstairs," she said. "Then I couldn't sleep, wondering what was wrong."

"Nothing necessarily is wrong," he said. "I did reset the alarm, so go back to bed."

She smiled and said, "I'll try to do that."

As she disappeared into her room and left the door open just a hair, he wondered if Bernie had gone into her room during the night. Or was she content to stay with him?

As he walked back to his room, he watched as Bernie looked at him, then looked at the door to the master, walked inside to check it out, and then came back to him.

"Good girl," he said. He suspected it would be quite hard if he took Bernie away from Addie. She's the only one who seemed to have cared about the War Dog. And Addie also still felt horribly guilty about her family's treatment of Bernie.

As he lay here quietly in the bed, he thought about all the things that had gone wrong... and right, wondering why, right now, *this* would come into his life. A woman he cared about. It was just such crappy timing. On the other hand, it was what it was. As always, he played the cards he'd been dealt, and, with that, he closed his eyes, dropped a hand to Bernie's head, patted her gently for a few moments, and fell asleep.

CHAPTER 9

A DDIE WOKE UP, got dressed right away, then she headed downstairs. She thought for sure she'd be the first up. Instead the kitchen's back door was open, and, as she stepped through, she saw Bernie in the yard, while Tucker sat on the deck. He looked up guiltily, a coffee mug in his hand, and said, "I hope you don't mind, but I put on a pot of coffee."

"Of course I don't mind," she said. "I'm just surprised that you're up so early. I thought you'd stay in bed for sure."

"No need," he said. "I woke up feeling great, so I decided to get up as usual. Besides, Bernie here needed to go out."

She nodded. "Did you leave any coffee?"

"I think there's a cup for you," he said.

"If not, I'll put more on," she murmured, as she headed inside to the coffeepot. She pulled a cup down and poured herself a cup to take out on the deck. She greeted Bernie, who'd come racing over from the backyard, and Addie spent a few moments just cuddling her. "Don't you look so much better, girl? I sure hated to see you in that pound. A beautiful girl like you does not deserve to be caged."

"I don't think any animal does," he said. "Never been a big fan of zoos either."

"I know," she said. "I'm of two minds over them because it's so nice to see the animals we don't always have a chance to see in any other environment. But I think caging them, even at the zoos, is cruel to the animals themselves, so what are you supposed to do?"

"We do the best we can," he said. "That's all we can do."

She looked up, smiled, and said, "You sure your head is doing better today?"

"It's doing much better," he said. "I'm pretty hardheaded as it is."

She smiled at that and nodded. "I've noticed."

He grinned.

"Plans for today?"

"I was wondering about going back to the job site, but I'm not sure," he said. "I'm ready—as ready as I can be—for the rehearsal later today and the wedding tomorrow. So whatever I want to do today, I need to get it tied up."

"And what does that mean for you?"

"It means I need to check out of the hotel," he said. "We'll be in Saint Pete's later today, and we'll stay at the hotel there tonight."

"Is there anything more you can do right now regarding Bernie's future?" she asked.

"Since I'm not trained to work with her, I need to talk to somebody about learning the proper orders to get her to work more efficiently," he murmured. "I don't know what Rodney's got in mind, as far as Bernie working for him. I'll talk to him in a little bit, when it's not quite so early."

But then his phone rang. He looked at it and frowned and said, "Apparently Rodney's up early too. "Hey, Rodney. What's going on?"

Addie sat there quietly, listening to Tucker's side of the conversation. "I know. I thought somebody was around here," he said. "Have you checked in with the police this morning to see if they found anything in the area? … Ah."

She frowned as she heard his tone changing. She realized that their discussion was about going back during daylight to see if they could find any clues surrounding the attack on Tucker. It wasn't a bad idea. It just wasn't really how she wanted to spend her day, but still she would rather be doing that than staying here and worrying.

When he finally hung up from the phone call, she asked, "Can I come?"

"Are you sure? It's that long drive again."

"Well, if we leave now," she said, "it wouldn't be too bad. And you're not going all the way to the site, right? Just to the restaurant?"

He frowned at that and then nodded. "No need to return to the arson site. At least I don't think so. Just the restaurant."

"In that case," she said, "we might as well have breakfast there. It's not that far away, and I can wait on breakfast."

He laughed. "Quite true," he said. "We can do that."

She grinned. "Then let's go." And, with that, she stood and said, "We'll hit the hotel on the way, so you can change your clothes."

"We can do that," he said, "and I can grab a shower and check out at the same time."

"So after we visit the attack site, we'll come back here to get ready for the rehearsal?"

Tucker nodded. "You got it," he said. "Okay, hotel first. Then a visit to the scene of the latest crime. That can take over an hour or two. But we're still good on timing to make it to the rehearsal."

TUCKER DROVE, EVEN though he was sore and tired, but he'd been in recovery for a long time now, and he valued his independence. He certainly trusted her to drive, as he had the previous night, but he felt just that much better to take the wheel himself. She didn't give him any argument, for which he was grateful. She trusted that he knew what he could handle and what he couldn't. Maybe because of that he said, "If you don't mind, I'll probably get you to drive home." She nodded. They arrived at his hotel soon afterward. "Do you mind waiting with Bernie, while I take a quick shower and change at my hotel room?"

"No problem. I'll take her for a walk."

True to his word, Tucker was back in less than fifteen minutes, and they all regrouped in his rental truck, with Tucker again in the driver's seat.

"It's probably a good idea for you to drive now, early in the day," she said quietly. "I get that you want to test how you are doing," she said, "but, by the end of the day, you'll feel it even more."

"Very true," he said. "Great painkillers though."

She laughed. "Modern medicine at its best."

"I didn't take the time to check out yet, and I didn't dare bring my suit with me. Not with all the attacks. We'll have to return for that." Addie nodded. He grinned and reached down a hand to nuzzle Bernie's head. "No contact with your sister yet?"

"No, not at all," she said, "and I'm okay with that too."

"Do you think she knows that the dog escaped the death chamber?"

"By now probably so. She's either plotting more, or she's giving up."

"And if she were to give up, what would that look like?"

"It would mean I would be suffering for a long time, if she had anything to do with that."

"So she thinks you're behind it?"

"I'm sure she does," she said, "and I'm okay with that too."

"And how much distress will this cause you?"

"I'm fine with whatever she does, as long as it doesn't hurt anybody else. I have to care to be hurt, and I'm pretty good at walking away from that drama now," she said with a laugh. "My sister is who she is, and I can't change that, but neither do I have to be around her to deal with it either."

"I agree. She has to understand how much she has brought on in her own life at this point."

"Except she won't care," Addie said. "When you think about it, all she cares about is what her life looks like. So the rest of it won't matter."

"Very superficial and selfish of her."

"You don't know the half of it," she said, laughing. "But again it's who she is, so not a whole lot I can do about it."

"Got it," he said. "Still sucks though."

"It does in a big way, but again she is who she is."

He heard her repeating that phrase over and over again, almost as if she hoped that she'd believe it eventually. But no way one walked away from a family member this manipulative and vicious as that sister of hers and came away unscathed. He could only hope that whatever they did in the end here would help Addie deal with the outcome in case of a fallout. "Hopefully she'll learn to change," he said.

"I wonder how long something like that takes?" she murmured.

"Probably a long time."

"Yeah, that was my thought too," she said. "And how

sad is that?"

"The restaurant turnoff is just up ahead," he said, and he looked down at the dog. "What got me into trouble last time," he said, "was the fact that I came out to check on the dog."

"Ah, right," she said, "so maybe ..." Then she stopped.

"What?"

"I was just thinking about me going in and picking up our breakfast and bringing it out. We could have some sandwiches or something, you know, maybe egg and bacon sandwiches."

"I'm okay with that." He took the turn off the highway and into the parking lot. As he pulled in and parked, he said, "I really like those."

"Me too." She smiled and said, "Good, I'll be right back." She stopped and looked at the dog and asked, "Do I need to get her anything?"

"Probably better if we don't," he said. "We fed her this morning."

With that, she nodded and walked inside the restaurant. He sat in the driver's seat, studying the parking lot. He was still trying to remember the little bits and pieces from yesterday, but, of course, the blow had come out of nowhere, and, when he'd woken up, he'd been out in the brush already. He looked down at Bernie. "It's okay, girl. We'll go take a closer look, but let's just wait for breakfast, okay?"

The dog barked once, and he cuddled her up closer. He took a long moment to scratch her under the chin, to rub the top of her head, to run smooth hands down her throat and her neck. He leaned over and gave her a big hug.

"You're such a sweetheart," he said. "I certainly understand that every animal will bite given the right circumstances, but it's hard to know what that circumstance would be in your case, if you didn't bite the psycho sister. But, if you do bite someone, I hope it is that nasty sister because she deserves a couple good bites. But even that thought just made you sick somehow though, didn't it? Just thinking about all that vile nastiness in your mouth was bad enough, huh?"

He continued to talk to Bernie gently in a soft tone, just giving Tucker time to stretch out and Bernie time to ease back a little bit. She seemed totally willing to listen to his voice to stay calm. No reason for her not to. No threats were around, no aggravation or arguments were happening to disturb her peace. Everything was very peaceful out here. He wondered if it was too peaceful or if just that inner sense he had said that his world was usually full of chaos and war. Not since he'd been hospitalized obviously but, before that, it seemed like all he had were various elements of strife, one way or another.

But not now. And that was important to hang on to.

As he sat here, musing about the changes in his life, the restaurant door opened, and Addie came back out, carrying a large bag and a tray of coffee cups. He rolled down the window and said, "I should have thought that you might need somebody to help you carry stuff."

"As you can see, I did just fine," she said with a smile, as she held out the few things in her hand. "If you'll grab the cups," she said, "I'll come around and bring the rest of the food."

He took the two cups, put them in the holders in the dash. She walked around, opened the door, and hopped in. Immediately Bernie snuffled all over the bag.

"No," he said, "Bernie, that's not for you."

She gave him the most soulful look in her eyes, and Addie laughed. "I might have picked up a sausage sandwich for her," she said.

He just rolled his eyes at her. "You know it's not good for her."

"A lot of things aren't good for her," she said, "but, at this point, I don't think that's the priority."

"I can't argue with you there," he said with a smile. He looked down at the dog. "You're already spoiled, that's all."

She gave a *woof* and laid down between them, her eyes like a hawk as they unwrapped egg sandwiches. Tucker took a bite, loving the taste of the sausage patty—even though he knew it was probably loaded in sodium and fat—but, for once, he didn't give a crap. "These are really good."

"I'm enjoying it too," she said, studying the sandwich in her hand. "It's funny the things that you end up liking."

"It works for me," he said. "Just think about how more traffic would benefit a place like this."

"It's also one of the reasons why I wouldn't come though," she said. "I prefer much less traffic than more."

"You and me both." He smiled, and the two of them kept eating.

By the time Addie was down to the last bite, she held it out to Bernie. She immediately whimpered and wagged her tail, inching closer. Addie gave it to her, then pulled out the extra sandwich for her. Bernie was very animated in her appreciation. The sandwich was gone in about two gulps.

Then Addie lifted her coffee, took a sip, and winced because it was still too hot. "How about we go take a look? Now that the food's gone, we can take the coffee with us."

"I was just going to suggest that," he said, popping his dirty wrapper into the paper bag. He held it out for hers and then hopped from the truck, letting Bernie out on his side. He reached for his coffee and walked up to a garbage can to dump their trash bag. He turned, hit the button on the key fob to lock up his truck, and then waited for her to catch up with him and Bernie.

"Are we expecting to find something here?" she asked.

"I hope to find something, but expecting? I don't know about that. It would just be nice."

"Great," she said. "I'll tell you where we found you but ..."

"No," he said, "show me where you found my phone."

She stopped, oriented herself, pointed in the right direction, and the three of them quickly followed that path. When they got to the edge of the parking lot, a cement barricade stopped vehicles from driving farther. She asked, "How did the guy carry you over this?"

Bernie was already sniffing the area.

Tucker bent down, took a look, and nodded. "One guy. A fireman's carry maybe. Or two guys. Even so, probably had to shuffle over this with the added weight," he said, "and then managed to lose my phone in the process and didn't notice because he or they were in such a panic."

"Still ... would have been easier for him to just attack you in the truck," she murmured.

"I wasn't actually in the truck at the time. Remember?" he said. "I'd already come outside to walk Bernie."

She gave a *woof* in agreement.

"Right," Addie said, "so maybe you were already walking the dog over here?"

He frowned, nodded, and said, "That's quite possible actually, and maybe I had my phone in my hand, and, when I went down, he wouldn't have noticed. It was getting dark out at that time. That makes the most sense of all," he said with a bright smile, looking at her.

She shrugged. "I'm not just some dumb bunny."

He burst out laughing. "You're nothing like a dumb bunny," he said, reaching out a hand. She hooked hers into his, and they carefully walked toward where he'd been found. Bernie was on alert the whole way.

CHAPTER 10

ADDIE NOTED HOW quiet Bernie was, how her ears twitched at every noise. She watched Tucker study the ground, looking for hidden signs that she couldn't possibly even recognize. She thought about asking him what he was looking for but figured it would just distract him. So she waited, as they made one pass, two passes, and then three passes, finally noting that they were moving outward from the main pathway a couple feet every time. "What do you expect to find on the outer edges?" she asked.

"Tracks," he said. "Most people don't take as much care on their way out as they do on the way in. They almost panic, trying to leave as fast as they can."

"And yet we're still walking the same pathway he took on the way in?"

"Only for the moment," he said. "I'll switch, and we'll start looking wider soon."

She nodded and waited and did exactly what he said, and then he came to a stop at a group of trees. "He stopped right here," he said. "Look at all these footprints."

She noted the flattened ground cover and saw it had been well trampled. "Or it could have been somebody else," she suggested.

"It's possible," he said, "but not likely, given the circumstances of what already happened here."

She frowned. "Meaning two unrelated crimes weren't likely to be committed at the same place at the same time?"

"Something like that," he said with a nod. "Plus see how Bernie is sniffing the area? She's got the scent of our guy."

She thought about it and said, "I guess that's a little bit too much of a coincidence, isn't it?"

"It is, and coincidences are not something that I'm very comfortable with," he said. "However, it's just supposition at this point."

"Right. I hear a lot of people talk about the fact that there is no such thing as a coincidence," she said, "but I have a hard time saying fate played a part in any of it either."

"You don't believe in fate?"

"Maybe," she said with a shrug. "I'm just not sure how much credence can be put into an unknown, unseen, unproven force."

"While acknowledging that you don't know something, what you understand is way better than being defiant about it one way or another," he said, "because I think everybody's opinion can change when new information comes to light."

"Well, I guess what I mean to say is, nobody's ever proven to me that fate actually exists."

"I can see that." He looked at the area and started taking several photos.

"You believe this is important?"

"Well, I don't want to take the chance that it is important later and just ignore it now," he said. "Better to do my due diligence at this time."

"Okay, can you tell where he went from here?" He pointed in the opposite direction than she expected. "Seriously?" She looked over there and said, "Nothing's there."

"Maybe, but that's where he went, and that's where we'll

go right now." He smiled at her. "Come on. Let's go."

She followed along, giving him some distance, so she didn't mess up any tracker trail that he seemed to think he was following. When they finally stopped, she looked around and said, "Oh, a road is here."

"And he probably took the road back to the restaurant and picked up his vehicle, so it looked like he was coming from a completely different direction and then took off," he muttered to himself.

"Is that a good deduction then or a bad one?"

"It just make sense," he said. "Again look at Bernie. She's picked up the same scent, I believe." He looked at Addie, smiled, and said, "No right or wrong. Just gathering theories."

"Ah." Again she didn't quite understand, but, if it made him happy and if it got them farther down the road to figuring out who and what was going on here, she was all for it. "I would like to figure out who did this," she said. "I'll have nightmares about you disappearing off the face of the Earth because I couldn't find you."

"But you did find me," he said.

"Only when we started calling for the dog," she said, looking down at Bernie. "She stayed quiet at your side the whole time."

"Yes, but, when I was attacked, she took off," he said. "Or went to the bathroom."

"Then she got confused with the other man or men with you, so she followed you here, or you ordered her to stay?" she said with a shrug. "Who's to say what went through the dog's mind at the time?"

He just nodded and continued to walk. As they arrived at the restaurant again, she noted they'd been walking for about ninety minutes. "Interesting to see that all of this evidence is still here," she said. "I guess if it had rained, all of it would have been gone, wouldn't it?"

"To a certain extent, yes," he said. "Certainly any rain washes away a lot of it, but, in the brush there, we don't see a whole lot of other tracks. So I don't imagine those tracks would have been affected as much because they would have been protected from the heavy rainfall."

"What about the dog? Can Bernie track the footprints?"

She looked at Tucker, as he looked at Bernie, shrugged, and said, "I'm not sure who and what to track. I don't have anything of the guy who knocked me out and kidnapped me, and she didn't show any kind of hostile reaction when we were at the location where you found me."

"Right," she said. "What about looking for the accelerant? Would she tell you if it was the same guys?"

"I don't know. We still must direct her somehow, so I can understand the results of what we're getting."

"Right," she said, feeling frustrated over the whole issue.

They stayed outside for another twenty minutes, walking near the restaurant, and she asked, "Do you see anything?"

"No," he said, stopping at the road his attacker left by. Tucker said, "Let's go back the same way we came in, and I'll take another look."

Bernie was happy to tag along.

"Why would you ever worry about anybody coming back here?"

"I'd be happy if he did," he said quietly. "It would give me a chance to fight him face-to-face."

"That doesn't make me any happier," she said.

He smiled, nodded, and said, "Sometimes it's what we need to do though. Fighting hidden enemies is almost impossible. You must look into the shadows, so that you can really see who you're fighting."

She nodded and stayed quiet. Bernie was much less excited about the smells this second time around.

As they walked back to where she found him, she shivered. "I don't like this place," she whispered. He stood up from his crouch, reached for her hand, and murmured, "The good news is," he said, "we don't have to stay here."

She smiled, and he grabbed her hand, and slowly they walked back. Just as they were about to leave the brush and to head into more of an open area back to the parking lot, she heard an odd noise, before she was suddenly slammed to the ground. As he dropped on top of her, she realized that odd noise she'd heard had been a bullet.

Bernie growled, searching the area.

"Don't move," he said against her ear. "Just stay where you are until I get back."

And then he bolted above her and took off. She laid frozen in place, watching as he and Bernie took off in the same direction. Addie knew he had to leave, but, at the same time, damn it, she didn't want to be out here alone. What if that shooter hadn't been by himself? What if, even now, he was coming toward her because he'd found another way to get here?

She lay on her back, too terrified to move, wondering what the hell was going on that they were even in this situation. She was grateful the dog was here to help, but, at the same time, she didn't want to be involved in this. As she thought that, she stopped because, if she didn't want to be involved in this mess, then what was she looking for from Tucker? If he would get into a mess like this again, did that mean she didn't want anything to do with him? She laid here, sorting out her confused feelings, when he suddenly returned. She stared up at him, and he smiled, reached out a hand. "Is it safe?" she asked.

"It is now," he said. "Did I get him? No. But did I get a picture of his vehicle? Yes, and I saw him bolt into the vehicle and take off down the road."

"Did he leave the way he left last time?"

"Yes," he said, "and that's how I found him."

"Right, because you knew the way he was going, so you jumped in ahead and got there first, so you saw the vehicle. Do you think he saw you?"

"I don't know," he said, helping her up to her feet.

She reached out a hand to pet Bernie, who looked like she was enjoying this. "Did you get hurt?"

"Nope," he said, but his fingers were busy texting on his phone.

She waited until they stopped. Then she looked up and said, "At least you don't need stitches again."

He laughed. "No," he said, "I'm fine."

"Does this happen a lot with you?"

Something must have been in her voice because he stopped to face her and then shook his head. "Honestly, no. I've led a very simple life since my accident."

"And before that?"

"Only on the job," he said, "but then it's what I was sent in to do. I knew who I was going after. I was with my team, well-armed and well-trained."

"And that makes all the difference, doesn't it?"

"It does, indeed." He gave her a searching look, reached out, and opened his arms. She fell into them, so grateful when they closed securely around her. "I'm sorry," he said. "I didn't even think about how shocking that must have been for you."

"I've just never been in anything like this," she said. "The only violence I've had any exposure to is from my sister."

"And she's bad enough," he said. "I'm sorry you had to get touched by this."

"It's okay," she said, trying to shake it off. But she was trembling.

He shook his head, held her that much closer, rocking her in place.

"So now what?" she tried to ask calmly.

"Now we'll head back to your place," he said. "The rehearsal's this afternoon, and we need to get there in time, and I need to make sure that the cops are picking up this vehicle."

"What if he ditches the vehicle?"

"I thought of that," he said. "I really hope he doesn't. That's also why I'm hoping that he didn't see me because that would give us a little bit more time to get in our vehicle and go after him."

"Do you know which direction he took?"

"Heading back the way we are."

"So then we will be following him? Is that wise?" she asked.

He nodded slowly. "Yes, but I also don't want him to know that we're after him."

She nodded, and the two of them walked back at a hurried pace but not a flat-out run. "Have you got somebody up ahead looking for him?"

"I do," he said. "The same cops from the arson case."

"Interesting," she murmured. "Well, let's hope they get him before anything else happens."

"That's the plan," he said cheerfully.

She finally eased back and said, "I'm sorry. I'm just not used to this."

"Don't ever apologize for that," he said. "Nobody should ever get accustomed to this level of violence. Nobody wants to," he said. "It's much too painful for everybody."

"I guess," she said with half a smile. "We just don't even think about violence to that degree, do we?"

"No," he said, letting the dog up into the front seat. He hopped into the driver's seat of the vehicle.

"You wanted me to drive," she said after a moment.

"Not a problem," he said, smiling.

"And still I would feel better if you want me to," she said.

He looked over and shook his head. "Not needed."

TUCKER SAW THAT Addie was quite shaken and with good reason. He had to leave her to track the other guy, and it had been worth it, but he'd also taken a gamble that could have put her in danger. Just even bringing her with him had put her danger. He wondered if it made sense taking her to the wedding. But just as he was about to argue that maybe she should stay home, she said, "I'm glad I'm going to the rehearsal and the wedding with you. It'll be something completely different this weekend to take my mind off this."

At that, he winced. "If you're sure you still want to?" he asked, shooting her a glance.

She looked at him, nodded, and said, "Yes. I mean it. Besides I like Rodney."

"He's a good guy," he said. "I need to update him too."

"Wasn't he supposed to be here?"

"He didn't make it yet. He's probably just running late."

"Maybe," she said with a doubtful tone. "An awful lot is going on right now. I think we're better off to make sure that he didn't get here before you."

"His vehicle wasn't here," he said by way of explanation, but he pulled out his phone, put it up on the dash, and hit the contact number.

As the phone dialed, she said, "As long as he's safe. I guess that is my concern."

When Rodney answered, he said, "Sorry. I'm not there yet." His voice was hurried and out of sorts.

"That's all right," Tucker said. "We came and took a look at the same location, just making sure that no clues were left behind."

"Was there?"

"Well, we got shot at," he said, "if that helps."

"Got what?" Rodney said, flabbergasted. "Seriously?"

"Yes," he said. "We're both fine. Bernie too. I went after him and saw him get into a vehicle. Do you know anybody who drives a small Honda Accord, an older model, in kind of a rust color? Like a dark orange-red."

"Yeah, it's one of my painters," he said. "Why?"

"The shooter got into that vehicle and took off," he said. "So, if you have a name to go with that vehicle, it would help us a lot."

"Jesus," he said. "I think it's Rural, but I can't guarantee that he was the one driving."

"Nope, you can't. That's okay because we should have answers pretty quickly."

"Says you," he said. "I hate to think he's involved in this. He's a nice guy."

"Call the detective," Tucker said, "and fill him in on Rural too because they're setting up a roadblock for him."

"Jesus," he said, "just when I missed something, all hell breaks loose."

"Why did you miss it?"

"Your sister had a meltdown this morning," he said, "prewedding jitters."

"Great," Tucker said, half under his breath, "not exactly something you can walk away from."

"No, especially not this morning. There was something about, you know, if I really loved her and that type of stuff."

"Sorry, man."

"I'm sorry I wasn't there with you," Rodney said. "Can't believe you got shot at."

In the background, Tucker heard his sister.

"Who got shot at?"

Tucker winced. "I'll let you go now."

"Chicken," Rodney growled. "You could talk to her and let her know you're okay."

"Well, you can tell her that I'm okay," he said, laughing. And, sure enough, he hung up. He looked at Addie. "See? He's fine."

"I'm glad to hear that," she said, shaking her head. "And I don't blame your sister for having prewedding jitters. It's a hard decision."

"I guess it is," he said comfortably.

"I've never been in that position, so I don't know. Besides, she must have a reason for taking as long as she has," she said, defending his sister.

He grinned. "Don't you worry. We both love her, no matter how many prewedding jitters she has."

She settled back. "I'm being foolish, aren't I?"

"Nope," he said. "You're cute when you're upset."

She snorted at that. "That line work for you?"

"Never tried it before," he said with another big grin on his face.

She sighed. "You haven't been close to getting married yet?"

"Nope, not at all. Never felt the urge. You?"

"I've never had any relationships that got that serious."

"I think it takes a special relationship to get there," he said. "You know? You either hit it off earlier or it doesn't happen."

"I don't know," she said. "I'd like to think that, for some people, they can grow into a long-term relationship that stands the test of time, but I just haven't had too much experience with it myself. My parents are very good at enabling each other, but I don't know that they're very good together," she said. "So it's not exactly been a plus in my book for a prime example of a happy and fulfilling marriage."

"Understood," he said. "I kind of want to meet them, out of curiosity, but I don't really want to meet them."

"I kind of want to see them and give them hell myself," she said, "but I don't want to. Dealing with their own relationship and with their manipulative daughter is something I've brought up several times, and I know that no good news comes from that."

"And it's not your problem," he said. "Just make sure your sister doesn't have any more animals around her, but, beyond that, not a whole lot you can do."

"She treats people the same way," she muttered.

"As long as she can control them, she does."

She smiled. "You do understand, don't you?"

"I do," he said. "That doesn't make it any easier on you."

"No, but at least you don't think I'm making it up. And you realize dealing with my sister is out of the question. I've had some friends who didn't understand at all why I wasn't jumping all over my sister every time she pulled this shit. They just didn't get how much trouble it was to deal with her."

"And with somebody who's so far off that line of normal," he said, "most people won't believe you anyway."

"Yeah, that's kind of where I'm at now," she said. "What's that up ahead?" she said, leaning forward.

"Looks like a roadblock." He pulled into the long line of vehicles and grabbed his phone, calling the detective. "I see you got a roadblock up?"

"Only at the outskirts of town," he said, "and several officers were already there at the scene of an accident," he said. "I wish I knew what I was looking for exactly."

"I gave you the description of the vehicle and the tags. I don't think he saw me, so he should be in the same small Honda Accord with the same tags. I don't know if you talked to my brother-in-law yet or not," he said, "but he knows the owner of the vehicle is Rural, and he's a painter who works for him. Just may not be the driver today."

"And you saw the shooter run into the vehicle?"

"I saw this man run into the driver's side and take off, and he was carrying a handgun."

"No sign of the vehicle yet. How would he know you were there in the woods again?"

"He must have had the house under surveillance and followed us to the restaurant," he said. "We did have an intruder in the backyard last night. But, between the War

Dog and security on the property where we stayed at last night, he got run off. It's possible he was there at the woods for the same reason I was—to make sure no evidence was left behind. It's also possible that my brother-in-law might have said something to somebody in his crew. We were talking about meeting at the restaurant this morning to look for any other signs from the attack last night."

"So maybe the shooter was doing the same thing," he said doubtfully.

"Maybe. I didn't see anything except for some footprints," he said.

"And maybe that's because he already picked up anything else."

"Well, he should be ahead of us. We're behind at least fifty cars in the roadblock," he said.

"I'm here," the detective said, "walking up the road."

Tucker opened his truck door and stood on the running board for a better view. "And look at that," Tucker said. "We have a small Honda Accord up ahead."

"The car is about seven away from me," the detective said. "Hang on, while I keep walking."

"Just take it easy," Tucker said. "Remember how I said he's got a handgun."

"As long as it hasn't been fired recently and he has a license for it, then he's okay," the detective murmured. "If not, that's a different story."

"You don't want him firing at you. I do have the dog though."

"What do you expect the dog to do?" the detective asked.

"Well, she'll certainly recognize him because they had quite a scene outside. He managed to get into the vehicle after she chased him."

"Huh."

"Not to mention the fact that, if he's got any accelerant in his vehicle or on his person or used any in the last twenty-four hours or so, I imagine she'll smell it on him."

"But we can't use that in a court of law."

"No, not yet, because I haven't been working with her long enough, and I don't have my registration or training for that kind of thing, but that doesn't mean we can't use it to coerce a confession."

"Well, it all sounds good in theory," he said, "but I'm looking at the vehicle from where I am."

"And who's in it?"

"A single male."

"Get backup," Tucker said immediately. "If he feels cornered, he'll likely shoot you." The detective hesitated, and Tucker said, "Screw this. I'll pull off onto the shoulder. I'm coming with the dog. Just hold tight."

True to his word, Tucker pulled the truck off to the shoulder and stopped and parked it at a spot on the shoulder that was a little wider, looked at Addie, and said, "I need to go."

"Go," she said calmly. He raised his eyebrows. She smiled and said, "It's what you do best. Go."

He grinned, grabbed the dog, and hopped from the truck. "Come on, Bernie. Let's go find this guy." Tucker stopped, leaned deeply inside the truck but couldn't quite reach Addie. However, she seemed to know what he wanted because she leaned over too, and it was just close enough that he could kiss her.

"I'll be back in a minute." And he turned, racing forward, coming up on the other side of the Honda, and he saw the cops surrounding the Honda. Tucker didn't know what they would do or how badly this would go, but he wanted to make sure he was there, just in case. As he approached, the driver stepped from the vehicle, hands in the air. "I don't know what you're talking about," he said to the cops. "I don't know anything."

They ordered him flat on the ground. He complied, but then, as he lay down, he twisted suddenly and pulled something from underneath his jacket and started firing. Several of the cops slammed bullets right back into him. He lay there, moaning in pain, when Tucker raced up with the dog. Bernie reached the gunman and immediately started barking and straining at the leash.

The gunman looked at her. "What the hell's up with that dog? Shut it up." He was holding his shoulder. "You didn't have to shoot me."

"We figured you're in for suicide by cop," one of the men said calmly. "What do you expect when you fire at us?"

"I didn't mean to," he said. "I panicked."

At that, one of the cops looked at the shooter's wounds, then at his boss and said, "He's not badly hurt, both in the same upper arm."

"Good, we need to get him to medical care, and I want him under wraps real fast," the detective said. "This asshole doesn't get to run away from this. Not this time."

At that, Tucker struggled to contain Bernie, who was definitely looking for a piece of the gunman on the ground. Since he was already injured and under wraps with the cops, Tucker walked the War Dog back to the shooter's vehicle. "Bernie, let's go to work."

His voice was clipped. He kept a short leash on the dog, and the dog seemed to immediately understand. She sniffed around the vehicle, and, when they got to the trunk, she immediately barked and sat down. He asked the detective, "Can you open up the trunk?"

He walked over, pushed the button, and the trunk popped open. What Tucker saw was not what he expected. He looked at the detective, nodded at the trunk, and said, "You've got bigger problems now."

CHAPTER 11

ADDIE SAT IN the truck nervously. It wasn't so bad in here; she could keep Tucker in sight, but then he'd disappeared quickly. She saw chaos and could hear gunfire erupting up ahead, but she hoped that, with all the cops, it wouldn't be gunfire at Tucker. She still didn't quite understand what was going on, but, when he returned about an hour later, she was more than ready to get answers. She looked at him anxiously. "You're not hurt?"

"Neither of us are," he said, and he opened the door to let Bernie in.

"What's going on? Who shot at us?"

"Well, the cops caught our gunman, and they didn't search him but ordered him to the ground. He managed to roll and fire on several of them."

"Did he hurt anybody?"

"No, but he took two bullets, one in the shoulder, one in the arm," he said. "They'll take him to the hospital, get him patched up, and charge him."

"And it's the guy who hurt you?"

"Well, I can't be sure about that. Hopefully we'll find that out during their investigation. I was really afraid they'd kill him, and we'd get no answers," he said. "But then I had Bernie here sniff out his vehicle. We found a whole lot more than we expected."

"What?" she asked, anxiously looking at him.

He turned, stared at her, his face grim. "A body in the trunk."

She gasped, the color fading from her cheeks. "Seriously?"

"Yes," he said. "Not exactly sure what's going on, but that's why he was fighting to get out of there."

"Damn," she said. "It's one thing to get caught on the suspicion of an attack, kidnapping, plus the arson, but it's a completely different thing to get caught with a body in your vehicle."

"Well, he can sprout all kinds of denials, but it'll be hard to get out of this one," he said.

"Do we know who it is?"

"I took a picture of the man's face for Rodney to identify. He said it was Raul, this guy is Rural's partner, on the painting crew."

"Great," she said, "so it's likely all related."

"Yes, we think so."

"But is Rural talking yet?"

"Not yet," he said. "But I think, for the moment, this is over with."

"Well, I hope so. How many other people can hate us so much?"

He laughed at that, started up the truck. As the traffic moved, Tucker pulled back into the line, and the traffic was free to go now that the roadblock was removed. Tucker waved and honked at the detective, as he stood there on the side of the road. Tucker pulled to the shoulder again. The detective walked over, and Tucker mentioned that Rodney had identified the dead man for them.

"Right, and the prisoner's talking already," he said. "He

didn't want to kill his buddy, but his buddy had put them in a terrible position because he'd accepted money to burn down the property. And, once the dog got there, the guy got afraid that the dog would know something, and then he would get charged, so he wanted to take you out."

"Great, so the two buddies, Rural and Raul, knocked me out and carried me into the woods? Then Rural killed Raul, leaving me behind? I guess I should be thankful for that. And then today Rural worried about evidence, returned to the crime scene, and shot at us?"

"It was an argument that got out of control. Anyway, that's the gist of the story at the moment."

"And it makes sense," Tucker said. "It'd be nice if we could tie up the arson and the attack at the same time. I just wonder how the hell they knew we would be there this morning."

"Not sure that he knew you would be there at all. But he was looking to see if his buddy had left any evidence at the scene that would incriminate him. When he saw you, he didn't know what to do but tried to go after you as well."

"Wow, he's just losing on all corners."

"Well, now he's injured, and he'll go to jail for a long time," he said. "You know a lot of charges are coming up for him, including firing on several police officers, but the murder charge will trump the lot."

"I don't care what trumps what as long as it's over," he said.

"You and me both. You and me both." He smacked the driver's side of the truck, where Addie sat now, and said, "Get ready for that wedding now."

"Right, Rodney will be beside himself if I'm late." Tucker waved and jumped into truck's passenger seat.

"It's just the rehearsal, isn't it?" she asked, as she drove.

"Yes, as far as I know," he said. "I don't even know why we need a rehearsal if it's a small wedding."

"Maybe they'll make it for real instead of a rehearsal," she said.

"I don't know. I think you need a minister for that."

"Maybe. You'd think after all this time that they would just take the chance and get it done."

They made it back to his hotel, and he quickly checked out. He got the rest of his stuff, threw it all into the back of the truck. They stopped at her place, where they could get showered and changed, with him in a suit and her in a sundress and sandals. By now it was midafternoon, and they headed to where the wedding rehearsal would be. It was a small church with a large park outside.

Rodney stood there nervously in a black suit too. "I don't know why we have to rehearse," he said, "I'm already terrified she won't show up as it is."

"She needs to," Tucker said. "This is a lot of stress on everybody."

"Did you have any thoughts about maybe instead of a rehearsal just getting married now?" Addie asked.

Rodney looked at her a moment, and then a slow smile dawned. "You know what? I like that idea. She's been trying to get out of this for a long time. When she finally agreed, she went through all kinds of panic about it."

"Well, if she knows this is only a rehearsal," Addie said, "she should be here today, but maybe you want to make it real instead of a rehearsal. Take the stress right out of it for her tomorrow."

Rodney laughed. "She might hate me for it too."

"It's hard to say," Tucker said. As they stood here, another vehicle drove up, and, sure enough, it was his sister. She hopped out, not in her wedding dress but a beautiful dress anyway. Seeing him, she ran forward to give him a great big hug. "You almost died," she said, "again."

"So can we finally get you married?" Tucker said. "Just in case I don't make the next attempt."

She gasped at him, and tears came to her eyes.

He groaned, pulled her into his arms, and said, "Sorry, that was a bad joke."

"It was a terrible joke," she cried out. "Why would you even say something like that? And today of all days."

"Because you've been giving Rodney hell about actually getting married," he scolded. "Come on. Let's get this done."

"It's not supposed to be something that we just *get done*," she said. "It's supposed to be something that's revered, that's honored."

"Do you honor him?"

"Of course I do."

"Do you love him?"

"Of course I do," she said in exasperation.

"Then what's the problem?"

Silence fell everywhere around them.

TUCKER DIDN'T KNOW how to make it any simpler than that, but sometimes his sister just needed straight-talking to.

She looked up at him, tears in her eyes, and she leaned in closer and whispered into his ear, "I'm pregnant."

He grinned at her. "Well, I'm delighted to hear that, but maybe you should be telling Rodney."

She nodded slowly. "I just didn't want the wedding to

happen because of this."

He rolled his eyes, turned to Rodney, and said, "Well, I'm hardly the person to break this to you," he said, "but it does explain some of the behavior that you've been dealing with for the last few days."

Rodney looked at him, then looked at his soon-to-be-wife in confusion. "What are you talking about?"

Addie understood. "Oh, my gosh," Addie said. "Congratulations."

Molly looked at Addie and smiled. "You must be Addie," she said.

"Yes, I am." Addie walked over and gave her a big hug, and then she walked to Rodney and said, "Congrats."

He looked at her in confusion and looked at Molly. "What is she congratulating me for?"

"You'll be a dad," Tucker said bluntly. "And that's why there has been emotional hysteria."

Rodney stared at Tucker for a long moment, his face blank, and then he looked at Molly. "Seriously?"

She nodded slowly. "And I started to panic."

He opened his arms, wrapped her up tight in a big hug, and said, "How could you possibly panic about us getting married?"

"Because I figured that, if you found out," she said, "then you would marry me just because I was pregnant."

He looked at her in confusion. "So you were trying to keep it a secret?"

"Then I felt guilty," she said. "So I've been torn as to what to do."

"Obviously you always tell me the truth," he said, "and then you'll get your pregnant ass in that church, and you'll marry me. I've been trying to marry you for a decade. Now this just makes me even more determined."

She burst out laughing. "I didn't know how you'd react."

"Well, you could have tried telling me and finding out," he roared. "I've had hell for a couple days now. But this is the best news you could possibly have given me."

"But what if I wasn't pregnant?"

He looked at her, shook his head, and said, "Don't even start. Now this is supposed to be a rehearsal, but they suggested that we skip the rehearsal part and just get married."

She looked up at them all in delight. "Is that possible?"

"Why don't we find out?" Tucker said. "At least we could get one thing accomplished today."

"Something I've been trying to get accomplished for a very long time," Rodney said, rolling his eyes. "I don't want to go through this anymore."

At that, the church doors opened, and the minister said that they were welcome to come in. Rodney walked in and took a few steps with him and had a quiet conversation.

Addie looked over at Molly. "Are you okay to get married today? You're not in your wedding dress."

"Honestly it doesn't fit," she said in a dull whisper. "I was still panicking over what I was supposed to wear." She shrugged. "I guess I overreacted."

"You never really wanted to be a mom," Tucker said cautiously.

"I didn't before," she nodded. "And then I did, and then I figured that I was too old, and it wouldn't happen, and Rodney didn't want any, and I just went down a rabbit hole."

"Wow," Addie said in fascination. "I guess talking to

him wasn't an option?"

"Yet he's the easiest person to talk to," Molly confessed. "I'm just an idiot."

At that, Addie burst out laughing. "No. You are not an idiot," she said. "You are pregnant, and it's your wedding day."

At that, Rodney came bouncing back with a big smile on his face. "We can do it right now," he said. "We have witnesses, and, other than that, we can just go and get this done. I'm not sure what to do about tomorrow, but we'll figure it out." He stopped, looked at Molly, and said, "Unless you've got other plans?"

"The only plans I have right now," she said in relief, "is to get married."

Rodney frowned. "We don't have any flowers, and then there's your dress."

"I know," she said, "so there might be a big bill for all that."

"Well, we didn't have very many ordered anyway, did we?"

"No, the expensive part is my dress."

"Right," he said, then straightened, took a deep breath, and offered, "You want to go home and get changed?"

Molly looked at Addie, then at her husband-to-be, and shook her head. "I was just telling Addie that my dress doesn't fit, and I was starting to panic as to what to do."

Rodney smiled and then started to chuckle. "Honest to God," he said, "I'm just so damn glad that this will happen right now. As long as you're happy, please let's go in and get married."

She reached up a hand and held it to his cheek and said, "I'm sorry."

"I'm not," he said. "I've always loved you, and now I have even more reason to get married."

"You're not upset?"

"No, of course not," he said.

"We didn't talk about it though. Having kids."

"We did early on, yes," he said. "Then it became one those things that I just figured you didn't want to have a family. Or at least not now."

"All of the above," she said. "Then I found out I was pregnant." Her hand went immediately and possessively to her belly. "And then I couldn't think of anything else."

"Good," he said, "because honestly that's the way it's supposed to be."

"Perfect," she said. "Do you have the rings?"

He pulled them from his pocket and said, "Yes." Rodney held out his hand to Molly and said, "Come on. Let's go."

When Molly accepted Rodney's hand, Tucker smiled and turned to Addie. "Then let's go." He reached out a hand to Addie and led her behind the wedding couple into the church.

And together Rodney and Molly walked in through the door, with Addie and Tucker behind them. He left the dog on her leash, secured to the truck's bumper for the short ceremony. The minister performed a simple yet sweetly moving ceremony, sealing their vows with a kiss, and, by the time it was done, everybody was incredibly thankful. Molly threw her arms around Rodney, kissed him wholeheartedly, and then turned to her brother, wrapped her arms around him, and just held him close.

"You see?" he said. "It wasn't a big deal."

"Why did I make it such a big deal?"

"Because it was to be special, and, as always, you wanted

it perfect."

"Well, I feel like a perfect fool," she admitted.

"Well, that's one form of perfect too," he said, laughing.

She grinned. "I'm really glad you're here. It's not the way I thought it would turn out, but honestly it's still probably the best way."

Rodney wrapped an arm around her shoulder, tucked her up close, and murmured, "Absolutely it is. We weren't having a big reception anyway," he said. "So I guess what we'll do is still keep the reception tomorrow?"

She nodded. "That's a good idea, and everybody will come for that part to celebrate with us."

"Exactly," he said. "We could announce that here and take care of that right now."

She nodded and smiled. "The reception was supposed to be at the hotel anyway, with a simple wedding beforehand."

"Well, the ceremony done now would mean the minister doesn't have to show up tomorrow, so that's a given," Rodney said. "I spoke to him about that, and he was fine with it." Rodney frowned. "I suggest the flowers come to the reception maybe a little earlier instead of the church, and then we won't have to worry about those either."

Molly nodded, all smiles.

Tucker felt something settle inside. A side glance at Addie showed the tears sparkling in the corner of her eyes. Something was so poignant about the way this wedding happened; … obviously it touched her as well. He squeezed her fingers. She immediately sniffed back tears but smiled at him, as she squeezed his fingers in return.

"You okay?" he murmured, watching his sister and Rodney accept well-wishes from all.

"Never better."

CHAPTER 12

AFTER THE CEREMONY the newlywed couple hugged their guests; then everyone headed to their vehicles to make the trip to Saint Pete's Beach hotel for the slated rehearsal dinner. Addie and Tucker took a moment to walk Bernie to a nearby grassy spot. The guests finally all arrived at the hotel for a nice semiformal dinner that night, where, again, Tucker tied Bernie's leash to a nearby bike rack on a grassy corner nearby. Since all the stress evaporated when the wedding plans had changed, everybody was much more relaxed, so it ended up being hugely enjoyable, even some of the guests going outside to interact with Bernie.

Addie got to know Molly quite well over their conversations. Having met Rodney several times, Addie had already formed a relationship there and that was much easier for them all. Turning to Molly, Addie asked, "Did you make all the phone calls to cancel what wasn't needed tomorrow?"

"I did," she said. "And it feels honestly much better, like I haven't been shackled."

"I'm surprised you were that much against marriage."

"I had a previous boyfriend," she said. "He hounded me and hounded me to get married, and every day that it got closer and closer to signing the deal, I got more and more panicky. Finally I told him the day before the wedding that I couldn't do it."

Addie winced. "I can imagine he was disappointed."

"Yes," Molly said with feeling.

"How bad was it?"

"I ended up in the hospital," she admitted. "It's one of the reasons why Rodney has never pushed me, and I appreciate that so much. But it did end up making me very resistant to the whole idea."

"Of course," Addie said. "I'm so sorry you went through that. It's tough to see the wrong side of humanity, isn't it?"

"It is, indeed." Molly beamed at her. "You're really good for him," she said. "Tucker seems to be much more light-hearted."

"It's been a pretty rough few days," Addie said guiltily. "I also don't know what he was like before this."

"I heard about what happened. Plus I understand that you helped him free the dog that he came to help. So now, I suppose, he'll go home after the weekend."

"Oh," Addie said, suddenly depressed at the thought.

"You're not ready for that, are you?" Molly exclaimed in delight. "Oh, I'm so happy you two have a connection."

Addie sighed. "No, I'm not ready for him to leave. He's very special," she said, lowering her voice. "I didn't expect to meet anybody in this scenario, but I obviously have, and now I have to deal with the consequences that he doesn't live close by."

"Are you tied to Miami?"

"Lord no," she admitted, "and I'd do a lot to head to a less-populated area of civilization. You know? Like an acre in the woods, five minutes out of town, would suit me."

"Me too," said Molly with a laugh, "especially now that I've got a baby." She put a hand on her tummy, marveling. "I never wanted to raise a child in the city."

"It's time to make the changes you want going forward. Now you're married to Rodney, and you are starting a family," she said. "Honestly you're one of the luckiest people I know."

At that, Molly looked at her, smiled, and said, "You're right. I need to reassess how different my life is right now. For a couple years after Tucker's accident, I didn't know if he would live or die."

"Was it that bad?" Addie asked.

"It was that bad," Molly said softly. "And worse was, he wouldn't let me come to him. He wouldn't let me help or even be there for him."

"He probably didn't want you to see him like that because you would worry, and he couldn't do anything to make you feel better as he needed to focus on his own healing."

"That was part of it, for sure," Molly said, "but he's also been very independent and doesn't know how to accept help," she said. "It's not hard to see how I also come by my own stubbornness, honestly."

Addie burst out laughing. "I think we all have that problem."

"I guess you've got your family problems, don't you?"

"You could say that," she said, shaking her head. "My sister's a piece of work."

"Well, hopefully at this point, the dog trauma is over and done with, and you can get on with a life separate from your sister."

"I hope so," she said with a smile.

"You'll enjoy the weekend here for sure," she said. "Now I will too. All the stress is over, and I can just relax—instead of being worried about tomorrow," she said in a teasing voice.

"Exactly."

At that, both Rodney's and Tucker's phones rang. Molly looked at the two men and frowned. Rodney held up his hand and said, "Let me just answer it," he said. "I won't be long."

Molly turned to Addie and said, "The men, when they get into work, it's really hard for them to shut off."

"I get you," Addie said, "but, with all the stuff that's been going on right now, it's probably a good idea for them to answer these calls."

"I suppose so," Molly said.

Addie watched Tucker's grim face as he nodded at something said to him on the phone. When he put it away, he turned toward her. "The guy escaped from the hospital."

She looked at him and said, "Rural?"

"Apparently they had two guards on him, but the one guard found the other guard slumped over an ER hospital bed, and Rural's gone missing."

"How's that even possible?" Addie cried out.

"A serious car accident, involving several vehicles, came into the emergency area, while they were still there. Rural took advantage of the chaos and multiple people moving around, diverting attention from him, giving him a chance to escape."

"Do we know where he's going?"

"Not for sure. He was muttering about me and the dog."

"Great," she said. "It's a good thing you're not going back to that first hotel."

"It's a good thing we're not going back to your place," he reminded her.

She winced at that. "That's not exactly what I want to

hear either. Does he know who I am?"

"I don't know if he has your name, but it's possible he tracked us to and from your place," he said. "We'll have to keep you safe until this guy's recaptured."

"Fine," she said. "We're staying here anyway, in Saint Pete's Beach, for the weekend, right?"

"Absolutely," he said. "The good thing is, we have a fun party to attend tomorrow in Tampa."

"I can just imagine the explanations required," she said, laughing. "The guests will be a little confused."

At her side, Molly groaned. "I didn't even think about that."

"Just make one email-blast announcement," Tucker said, "telling everybody there's been a change of plans—in that you already got married—and tomorrow you're celebrating the wedding."

"That works," she said. "I honestly don't care anymore." She gave a one-arm shrug. "Now that it's over, I'm okay with whatever."

Her husband just grinned at her. "See? It wasn't that big a deal."

"It's supposed to be a big deal."

"To us," he said, "but it doesn't need to be a big deal to anybody else. It doesn't need to be some big showcase. It doesn't need to be a big parade. It should be exactly what it was. We tied the knot because that's what we wanted to do."

She's smiled. "You're really not upset about the pregnancy?"

"Of course not," he said. "How can I be upset? I was partly responsible for it."

"Sure," she said, "but you know life isn't always that neat and clean."

"It's never that neat and tidy," he said. "That's not a reason to avoid things."

"Okay," she said meekly. "We'll do this together." And she hugged her husband, a happy smile on her face.

The rest of the evening flowed with good conversation and lots of wine, although Addie found it a little harder to ease back her anxiety, knowing that the gunman had escaped. They got Bernie and drove back to their hotel, glad that the management allowed dogs. When the three of them finally made it to the hotel room later that night, she found double queen beds, even a doggie bed for Bernie, and she flopped down on the closest queen bed and asked, "Did you get an update yet?"

"I'm just texting the detective now," he said. He looked at her and asked, "Do you want a shower?"

"I wouldn't mind," she said. "Although I was wondering about a trip to the pool."

"We can do that if you want," he said. "We might as well make use of the amenities."

"I always wanted a pool," she said. "Something I just never managed to make happen."

"Well, it's not like you've had a whole lot of time to get there."

"Nope, I haven't," she said. She got up, grabbed her bag, and said, "You'll join me in the pool? And Bernie can come too."

"Absolutely, the manager said something about a special pet-only pool specifically for dogs," he said. They both changed, grabbed a towel. As the trio headed together to the pool, she said, "You know what? In a funny way, it was a nice wedding."

"It was the best," he said. "Nice and calm and quiet, no

nerves."

"I hadn't realized how nervous she was."

"And she's gotten worse now that she's pregnant."

Addie smiled and nodded. "Pregnant women do tend to be a little more neurotic."

"In this case, I don't mind," he said. "Not only do I finally get a great brother-in-law, who I think is the best husband for her, but I also get a niece or a nephew. And that'll be fun."

"Are you staying around then?"

"Rodney and I were talking about that earlier," he said. "He wants to move her out of the city, and she wants to go to a smaller town, where they can raise a family now. He'll spend some time looking into real estate to find a nice family home."

"And what about you?"

"Well, that's one of the things. You know when you reconnect with family, how it's hard to let go?" he said. "I'm not sure I want to let go of that connection now."

"I wouldn't want to, not with the loving family you have," she said. "Family can be tough, but they're also one of the best things for us."

"I hope so," he said. "It's the start of my new life."

At the pool, Tucker found the pet-friendly accommodations and got Bernie situated, already splashing water everywhere. He chuckled at her innocent joy. Addie looked on with a big smile and dropped her towel over one of the chairs and stepped into the cool water. "Something's so magical about being outside in a pool under the open sky. Too bad your sister isn't here to enjoy this. Do you think they've gone to sleep?"

"Probably. My sister was exhausted. She didn't have any

alcohol, being pregnant, but she was still tired, with the baby already taking a lot out of her right now," he said. "Plus they are newlyweds, so I would imagine they are in bed."

"Good," she said. "She'll feel that much better tomorrow."

Tucker slipped into the water beside her and stroked out strong in the darkness. Between the water and the lack of light, she couldn't see any of the injuries that he had already told her about, but she knew that they were there. Following his lead, she dove into the water, coming up on the other side, and struck out strongly for the far wall.

After she did ten lengths, she curled back up on the step in the shallow end and just stared, her face up to the sky, enjoying the stars.

"It's beautiful, isn't it?" he murmured.

"It so is," she said. "In the morning we should go down to the beach. Bernie will love that."

"We will, unless you want to go tonight," he asked.

"No," she said, "Bernie seems fine in her pool, and I can see the ocean from here. The waves are magical, and the beach reaches as far as the eye can see. Plus I don't want to leave here right now. It is just so lovely in this pool. It's really quiet," she said. "I expected it to be much busier here at the hotel."

"Maybe not this late in the evening. Tomorrow in Tampa will be a lot busier," he said. "All of Molly's friends and others will arrive at the reception there because Molly lived in Tampa for a long time. Molly and Rodney will probably end up there."

"It won't matter where, as long as she has her privacy and some land," she said. "They'll work it out. They have lots of decisions to make, and that's okay too."

"Very true," he said, "as do I."

"True." She nodded.

Tucker checked out Bernie, finding her resting peacefully now in the water of the little kiddie pool, her head laying on the soft edge. "What about you?" he asked, leaning back beside her, not touching, just quiet beside her.

"What about me?" She twisted slightly so she could face him.

"Are you staying in Miami?"

"No," she said, "not anymore. Not after this latest mess with my family. I don't want to be geographically close to them. I want to get out of town. Go to a place that's a whole lot less *city.*"

"Sounds like you want what Molly wants."

"To a certain extent. I'm not sure I'm ready to start a family though." She smiled. "What about you?"

"She and I always talked about having an acre apiece on the same block where we could walk back and forth to visit each other. When it's just the two of us, you plan things like that, in the hopes that, maybe, one day, it will come true."

"I think you have to *make* things like that come true," she said, "and this is an opportunity for you to do that."

"Maybe," he said, "it's a matter of finding the right place."

"Well, with Rodney being in property development," she said, "that shouldn't be all that hard. You'll have to look for two properties close to each other."

"Maybe." He smiled at her. "It's been a strange couple days, hasn't it?"

"So strange," she murmured, "but a lot of good came out of it."

"Like?"

"Well, your sister for one," she said. "I hardly know her, and yet I feel like I know the whole family."

He burst out laughing. "It's like that sometimes."

"In this case definitely," she said with a bright smile. "I don't think I've clicked with as many people as quickly ever in my life before. And it shows me a different type of sister."

"Rodney's a good person, and so is my sister," he said, "although she looked a little ditzy and lost it today."

"And she's allowed," she said, chuckling. "It was her wedding day, and she was pregnant and hadn't told her fiancé."

"That still blows me away."

"She was big enough already that she didn't fit in her wedding dress," she said. "I wonder if she's checked to see if she's carrying twins or not."

"Now that would be a handful," he said, and he started to laugh. "But it couldn't happen to nicer people."

Addie loved that about him. He was open, honest, and definitely one of those keeper kinds of guys. She smiled at him. "So does that mean you'll stay local?"

"Thinking about it," he said, "a whole lot more reasons now to stay local." He reached out a hand and gently stroked her wet cheek. "It'd be nice if we could stay in touch, could stay close," he said.

Her smile was gentle. "I was thinking the same thing," she said. "Whatever has been happening here between us has happened so fast that I wasn't exactly sure where we stood."

"I'm not sure where we stand either," he admitted. "But, having the serious injuries I've dealt with makes you realize waiting for tomorrow is no good—because sometimes the tomorrows don't come."

"It's a hard lesson, isn't it?" she said. "Sometimes it

makes me feel like I'm being greedy because I want everything now."

"I don't think it's that so much. I appreciate the fact that some days just don't go the way that you expect them to go, and you want them to be a whole lot easier, yet life has other plans," he said. "Losing our parents when we were young wasn't easy either. We've had to adjust to so much that I think, unlike my sister, I wanted all of it now too."

"Meaning *all*, as in marriage and a career and a family?"

"You know something? I think that would probably be a really good idea," he said, chuckling. "But the marriage or family is a little too early."

"I don't know," she said. "Depends if you have a partner tucked away somewhere that I don't know about."

"Nope, no partner tucked away somewhere," he said. "But, if you'd like to sign up for the position, just let me know."

She looked at him slyly, and then she grinned. "Is there a job application and an interview process for this?"

"Well, I wasn't thinking about it before," he said. "However, that interview process could be fun."

He slid his arms around her waist and stepped in between her legs as she sat on the top step in the pool. She wrapped her arms around his neck, as he lowered his head and gently kissed her. Their lips were cool from the nighttime swim, but the fire inside was anything but that. She gasped, as he finally raised his head.

"You are lethal," she muttered, trying to regain her breath.

"I don't know," he said. "I think I need another taste." And he lowered his head again, pulling her tightly against him. Ever mindful that they were out in public, she tried hard to restrain herself but couldn't. He lifted his head, then slanted his lips back down again and again. She shivered in his arms; he tightened his grip and whispered, "I don't want to push you."

"I'm not sure either of us is pushing, given the heat between us," she murmured against his lips. "But we're definitely not in the right place."

He pulled himself back and looked around, as if suddenly realizing where they were. "Right," he said. "Not a pool in our backyard," he murmured. He lifted his thumb and gently stroked her bottom lip. She nibbled on the end of his fingertip and then pulled it into her mouth, where she could suck it.

Immediately his eyes darkened, and she could feel the response from his body. She pulled back, scrambled to her feet, grabbed her towel, and said, "Meet you and Bernie back up at the room." And, laughing, she ran ahead of him to their room.

Inside she headed for the shower but left the bathroom door open, stripped down, placing her soaking wet bathing suit in the sink. She stepped under the hot water and gave a little shriek when warm hands handed her a bar of soap. She looked over her shoulder to find him standing completely nude behind her. His eyes dark, his face questioning, she smiled, turned around, hooked her arms around his neck, pulled him down, and kissed him hard. "I think you'd do a better job with the soap than I would."

"I'll do my best," he whispered.

And immediately he moved the bar gently but surely around her body from the underside of her chin right to her toes. She gasped in delight, shivering with passion as he moved upward again. He slowly stroked his hand up the inside of her calf to her thigh, stopping at the nest of curls. As he slipped his fingers between the plump lips, gently entering her, she moaned, separated her legs, giving him more access, and now leaned against the wall. "I don't think this will work," she gasped.

"Oh, absolutely it'll work," he growled in a husky voice, as he lifted her waist high and pinned her against the wall. She rested at the perfect place. She wrapped her legs around his hips, and he slowly, ever-so-slowly entered her. She shuddered in reaction, twisting at the overwhelming fullness.

He whispered, "Are you okay?"

She gasped and nodded. "I'm fine," she said, "but dear God."

"I know. Me too." He lifted his hips and plunged, withdrew, then plunged again and again, the water splashing all around them. Yet his arm held her firm, while his other hand was pressed securely to the shower wall.

Pinned against the back of the shower, she felt completely imprisoned and yet so close to a freedom that she'd never experienced before. She wrapped her arms around his neck and tried to move, but her rhythm wasn't in synch with his, making it worse, until finally she relaxed against the wall and let him set the pace.

He drove her harder and higher and faster than she thought she could even possibly go. When she flew off the cliff, she collapsed in his arms, a surge of emotions filling her. He plunged deep one more time, grinding his pelvis tight against her, before he slowly lowered them to sit on the side of the bathtub, holding her still in his arms.

"My God," she whispered. "I thought you said you were injured."

"I was," he said gently. "I think I said I was much better,

didn't I?"

When a cold nose hit her warm thigh, she gave a small shriek, only to see Bernie sitting there outside the shower curtain, her tongue lolling to one side. Addie reached out a wet hand and gently stroked the dog. "And, of course, you're here too," she said, "and somehow that just makes it all the more perfect."

He kissed her hard for that. "I didn't expect to meet anybody of the same mind-set."

"I know," she said. "It's just so very strange, isn't it?"

"Strange and yet wonderful." He looked at her and said, "What about your hair? Do you need to wash it?"

"I do," she said. "The chlorine from the pools is deadly."

"Got it," he said, gently disengaging. He turned the water a little bit warmer and quickly shampooed her hair, taking great care as he dispensed suds along the full length.

"I love that feeling," she murmured, as he gave her a gentle head scrub. By the time she had her hair washed twice and conditioner on, she asked for the soap. "My turn." And gave him a cheeky grin.

With his eyebrows up, he handed it over, and she quickly worked her way all over his back, down his buttocks, to his muscular thighs. When she came to the prosthetic, she asked, "Is that allowed to be in water?"

"Yes, even in the pool," he said. "Regular water is fine, if I'm wearing it. This is a special design by my boss's wife, made specifically to look lifelike," he said. "The chlorine can be bad for long periods, without rinsing it all off with soap and water. So a hop in the shower after pool time is recommended."

She continued her ministrations to his front, taking gentle care of his growing erection. "Nice," she said impishly.

"I'm okay to carry this into the next room."

And, with that, she gave his huge erection another silky slide up and down, before stepping back and out of the tub. She grabbed one of the big bath sheets, quickly toweled off, and then handed him the spare. In the next room, she pulled back all the bedcovers on one bed. Their bags were on the other, and she stretched out on her back. He came in and asked, "Are you ready for bed?"

She grinned at him, invitingly, then sat up on her elbows. "Do you think Bernie has to go back out again?"

He hesitated. "I should take her out. Hold that thought." He dressed quickly, gave her a smoldering kiss, then slipped out.

While she waited, she curled up on her side of the bed, completely uncovered, loving the heat, the warmth, but also the coziness of just being with somebody special. She barely heard him as he curled back into bed with her, and then he murmured against her ear, "Do you need to sleep?"

"Just for a little bit," she said. "Catch me in five."

She closed her eyes and drifted off.

TUCKER WAS DISAPPOINTED to not be resuming the activities that had just gone before. It was one thing to come together once, but he didn't want to hold it to that. He wanted to do so much more with her. As he lay here, his head back, the dog relaxed on the floor beside him, Tucker realized how far the three of them had come in such a short time. And, sure enough, only a few minutes later, she rolled over, looked up at him, and yawned.

"Couldn't sleep?" he murmured.

She smiled. "I power nap," she said, sitting up on her knees. She looked at him, grinned, and said, "Now, where were we?"

His heart leaped with joy, as he raised his arms above his head to lay them on the pillow. "I'm pretty sure," he said, "you were about to do something to me that was absolutely heartbreakingly and dastardly lovely," he said with a confusion of adjectives.

She chuckled out loud. "Maybe," she said, her hand sliding over his long length. "And maybe I would just explore this beautiful prime example of male flesh in front of me."

"Feel free," he gasped, as her hand closed around him again. "Do with me as you will."

"No arguments?"

"Hell no," he said, groaning as she slipped her hand up and down, squeezing, stroking, coming over the tip with her thumb, his hips already surging.

"I do see that you're tense though."

"Absolutely not," he said.

She leaned down, kissing his nipples. "Anything I do, I promise," she said, "I'll make it good."

And make it good she did. By the time they were done with this second round, he was the one shuddering in place. He groaned. "I think you finished me."

"That's good," she said. "It's supposed to relieve stress. But now I need to sleep."

"We both do," he said firmly. He reached a hand down the side of the bed to find Bernie's muzzle reaching up. He smiled and whispered to both his ladies, "Go to sleep, baby. Go to sleep."

And he closed his eyes and did the same.

CHAPTER 13

W HEN ADDIE WOKE the next day, she hadn't realized just what a fun outgoing day it would be. They ended up meeting the newlyweds for breakfast, going to the beach at lunch, and then attending the reception held in Tampa that afternoon. It went all through until dinner, which was part of it. By the time it was over, and everyone said their goodbyes, she and Tucker had been firmly encapsulated and introduced as a couple. Addie was fine with that, and the wedding couple appeared to be okay with it too. Matter of fact, Addie was more than fine with it, and, throughout the entire day, Bernie had been at their side.

Finally it was their turn to say goodbye. Tucker and Addie walked over to Rodney and Molly.

"We'll head back now," Tucker said. He leaned over, kissed his sister, shook hands with his brother-in-law, and said, "Welcome to the family again, not like you need it after all the years you've been there for us," he said. "I'm just glad you finally got this done."

"Me too," Rodney said. "Also keep an eye out because, as far as I understand, Rural's still not been caught yet."

"Not a problem," he said. "We'll keep a close eye. You too." At that, Tucker and Addie and Bernie hopped into the truck and headed back to her house. When they finally neared her place, she said, "Do we need to pick up any groceries?"

"You have to work in the morning, don't you?"

"I do," she groaned. "I don't like working for a living."

He burst out laughing. "I think most people would agree with you there," he said, "but it is a necessary evil. Unless you find your dream job."

"I guess," she said in a disgruntled voice. "Too bad I don't have enough money where I could just stay at home."

"And then what?"

"I don't know. I guess that's the question, isn't it? I'd be bored stiff."

After they parked, she hopped out, stretched, and said, "What a hell of a weekend."

"But a good one."

They walked to the front door, busily talking about how the reception had gone and how much fun it had been. She pulled out her key, turning it, only to wonder if the door had already been unlocked. She stepped inside without saying anything about it and froze. Tucker came in behind her and froze right by her side. Immediately Bernie started barking.

"Shut the dog up," the gunman snapped, holding the gun on her sister, who sat frozen on the couch. "Shut her up, or I'll shut her for you."

Immediately Tucker put a hand atop the dog, easing her back. "It's okay, sweetheart. Take it easy." Bernie's butt hit the ground, and she sat there, growling deep in the back of her throat.

Addie moved forward. "You must be Rural. What are you doing here with my sister?" she asked the two of them.

Her sister glared at her. "I can't believe you're the one who went behind my back to save that stupid dog," she said. She turned to the gunman and said, "The least you could do after the way you've treated me is to shoot it."

He shook his head and asked, "What have you got against the dog?"

"It hates me," she said, sneering. "It also bit me."

"Well, maybe that's a good thing," he said. "From everything that's come out of your mouth since I've been here, it doesn't sound like there was a whole lot to like about you." Before Bernie could speak again, Rural ordered Addie, "Get over here." Her sister glared at Addie, while the gunman waved at Addie. "Hurry up."

She looked at Tucker, who pulled her toward him, while Tucker slammed the front door hard. He glared at the gunman. "You haven't had enough yet?"

Rural snarled. "It's because of you guys that I'm here. What the hell were you doing at the restaurant?"

"Same thing you were," Addie said, stepping in front of Tucker. "We were looking to see if you or your partner had left any evidence behind."

"He was such an idiot," he said. "Now I'm the one left to pay the price."

"If you hadn't fired at the police, it wouldn't have been so bad," she said, "but maybe not, since you killed your partner."

At that, her sister stood and gasped. "You killed someone?" She glared at Rural. "What kind of asshole are you?"

He glared back at her. "Shut the fuck up and sit down."

She sneered at him. "Or what?"

In a fit of temper, he turned the gun and placed it against her temple. "Or I'll pull the trigger, just like I did with my partner."

The color left Bernie's face as she slowly sagged in place. She looked at her sister. "Addie, you won't let him talk to me like that, will you?"

Addie stared at her sister. This was so bizarre. Then everything with her sister was full of drama. The gunman was one thing—and should have been the biggest issue—but, true to form, her sister was making this all about her. "I doubt I could stop him, since he's the one with a gun. Besides, what are you doing here?" she said. "And how did you get in?"

Even Rural seemed interested in the family conflict playing out here.

"I used Mom and Dad's key, of course," she said. "They're not home anyway."

"You used their key. I get it, but why? You've never been here before." Maybe if Addie kept the gunman distracted, Tucker could find a way to get the gun away from Rural without anyone getting shot. But her sister was involved, … so all bets were off.

"I came a few times when you first moved in," she said. "It's awfully tiny though." Her sneer and bravado were back again. She looked at the gunman. "Don't you think so?"

He shrugged and said, "It's okay."

Bernie couldn't believe it. "Are you serious?"

"You just walk into my house when I'm not home? So you can what? So you can criticize it?"

"Why not?" she said. "It's not like you were answering your phone."

Addie shook her head, her hands on her hips. "What did you need this time? Somebody to run get you a coffee?"

At that, the gunman snorted.

Her sister looked at her and frowned. "No," she said, "I needed cream."

"Well, if you can manage to get here, you're capable of

getting your own cream," she said in exasperation.

"Oh, and our parents called," she said. "They're coming home this weekend."

"Great. What's that got to do with me?"

"I told them what had happened about the dog and that you were angry at me."

"I'm always angry at you. Nothing's changed there. You tried to kill a dog that did nothing to you. You treated it horribly. You abused it constantly," she said. "The best thing for that dog was to get away from you."

"That's not true," she snapped, glaring at the dog. "I hate it."

"Too damn bad," Tucker said beside Addie. "You have no rights to this dog now. It's mine."

She sneered at him, then spoke to Addie. "What'd you do? Pick up a hero while you're out? Men like that are easy," she said. "The trick is to get one with staying power."

"You're hardly one to talk," she said. "If you can't use and abuse, you don't give a damn."

Her sister looked at her in surprise.

Tired and fed up, hoping Tucker had a plan for the gunman, Addie snapped at her sister. "What are you here for?" she repeated. "And give my key back."

"I don't know what you're going on about," she said. "I just came for a visit."

"No, you didn't. You probably contacted your friend at the pound, and he told you that I had something to do with the dog's release."

"You had no fucking right," her sister said in her mean dictator voice, her face twisting with fury. "That damn dog needs to die." She looked over at the gunman. "I'll give you one hundred bucks to kill it right now."

He shook his head, looked at the dog, and said, "I still don't get what's wrong with the dog."

"She doesn't like my sister," Addie said in a dry tone. "That's all my sister cares about—herself. She wants it killed for that reason alone. She would torture the dog when it was sleeping and hit it with a chair."

Rural looked at Addie in shock and then looked at her sister. "Seriously?"

"I was hoping it would die," Bernie said.

"She used to starve it. Or she'd pour cleansers in her dog food," Addie continued. "There's nothing good about my sister's behavior to this dog—or to people for that matter."

"It sounds like the only one who should be getting a bullet is her," Rural said with a sneer, waving his weapon in Bernie's face.

Bernie bounded to her feet and walked up to the gunman, pushing him against the wall. "Don't you talk to me like that," she snapped.

He quickly pushed her back. "Hey, bitch. That's not too smart, since I'm the one with the loaded gun."

"I don't give a shit," she said, poking her finger into the gunman's chest.

He backhanded her with his free hand, the noise echoing, hanging in the air, as Bernie stumbled, grabbing at anything to keep from falling.

Bernie seemed affronted. "Don't you talk to me," she said, pouting now. "You have no idea how bad it's been. That dog hated me ever since I first got it. I begged my parents to get the dog, and then, when we get it, the dog hates me. So I decided it would pay," she said, now her hurt turning into anger. "It's not my fault. I wanted to make sure it suffered. So I filed a complaint. It should have been put to death yesterday, except for these two." She turned, looked at her sister and Tucker. Gave a clipped nod and snapped at the gunman, "Actually I'll pay $300," she said, "to shoot them all."

TUCKER STARED AT the sister and wondered about the severity of her psychoses. He had his phone in his hand in his pocket and had turned it on to video as soon as he saw the two intruders. Even though the video would only show the inside of his pocket, his phone would at least record their words.

"Wow," Tucker said, "you take the cake. It's totally about you, isn't it? Nothing matters as long as you get what you want, huh?"

"That's the way life is," she said with a disdainful look at her fingers. "There are users and losers."

"No," he said, "that's not the way life is. You're not supposed to sit here and just take everything you want in life. You're supposed to help others."

"No," she said in a languid tone, and she walked past the gunman, completely nonchalant about the gun in his hand.

Tucker was stunned because, given an opportunity, he would have removed the gun and, therefore, the threat from the guy altogether, but Bernie, who had the opportunity, didn't even care. She didn't even consider it. Didn't even think about it, not for her own self-preservation or for anybody else's. He figured she wasn't like Rural, expecting suicide-by-cop earlier, although this would be suicide-by-intruder instead. Nope. Tucker figured she never had to do anything for herself, including saving herself from ... herself and armed intruders.

He shook his head. "You're unbelievable," he murmured.

She smiled at him and said, "Thank you."

"Unbelievably evil."

She huffed and sat back down on her chair. The gunman waved the gun at her and said, "Now stay there." She just looked up at him and flicked her fingers, as if to say, *Piss off,* and ignored him. The gunman looked over at the two of them. "I feel sorry for you," he said. "She's a total bitch."

"She's always been like that," Addie said, her voice tired. "When my parents get back, she'll wrap them around her fingers and make their lives miserable too."

"They're not miserable," she said. "They love me and will do anything for me."

"But you don't do anything for them," Addie said, hating the truth of her words. "Even worse, you make their life something they don't want. Why do you think they take off on trips all the time?"

"Well, of course they do. They want to travel a lot."

"Instead of kicking you out of their home, they do it to get away from you," Addie snapped. "You aren't even adult enough to move out and to support yourself."

"Of course I could move out, but why would I? I mean, I'd have to pay rent and other bills, plus look after myself and cook." She snorted. "Until I can afford to have maids, I'll stay home," she said. At the word *maids,* the gunman stared at her in shock.

Tucker nodded. "Isn't she something?"

"Jesus," Rural said, "I pity the poor bastard who hooks up with you."

She glared at him, her voice like ice when she said, "I

make their lives wonderful," she said. "But I'm looking for one who's wealthy enough. Some of them have been close, just not quite enough there yet. I don't intend to work for a living," she said with a sneer, glaring at Addie. "That's for the lowlife laborers."

"Well, it's certainly for the everyday Joe," Tucker said with a note of amusement. Something was just so farcical about this whole mess. ... He shifted to one side and realized that the dog hadn't let her gaze off the sister. He reached down and whispered to Bernie, "It's okay. She won't hurt you anymore."

"Hell yes, I will," she said. "This guy'll shoot the two of you. Then I'll beat the shit out of the dog," she said, "and maybe, maybe then, when I'm tired, I'll let him shoot it."

Addie looked at the gunman. "So do you take orders from mentally ill women, like her?"

The gunman shook his head. "Hell no," he said, "that's the last thing I'll do. Besides, I don't shoot dogs, and obviously this dog's got more smarts than you have." He sneered, looking right at Addie's sister.

Bernie bounded to her feet again, raced over, and smacked him hard across the face. Instantly the gunman pushed her back, resuming some of his feistiness, but he'd lost his momentum amid all the psycho drama going on here. Tucker was already on Rural; Tucker had a hand against his throat, pinning him, as he grabbed the gunman's wrist, slammed it against the wall behind him, so that the gun couldn't shoot anyone. Hearing the growling behind him, Tucker turned to see the dog, sitting on her butt, glaring and growling at Bernie, the sister.

She looked at the dog, sneered, and kicked her.

"Don't do that," he warned her. "That dog answers to

me now, not you."

"I don't give a shit," she said, rising to join the fray. "Give me that goddamn gun." And she tried to wrestle it away from Tucker. What was going on was ludicrous; he wanted to punch the hell out of her and knock her out as it was. Addie grabbed her sister, pulling her out of the scenario, and forced her into the chair.

"Now stay there, damn it," Addie said. "You can't even see the seriousness of this situation."

"Well, I see what I want to see," she said, "and I see a gun that would take care of the job right now. There isn't even a law," she said, "that would charge me for this. The dog has already attacked me. Now it's glaring and growling at me," she said. "So I could get away with it, and it would not be a big deal."

Tucker, now holding the gun, pushed Rural into another chair.

The gunman stared at Tucker and then at Addie. "She's really not all there, is she?"

"She hates the dog, and she hates people, and, if she ever got good enough to start killing people, we'd have a serial killer on our hands like you wouldn't believe," Tucker muttered. "I've seen the type too many times in the military."

The gunman swore. "I don't want anything to do with her," he said. "She's damn scary."

"And, if you were smart," Tucker said, "you would fess up to the cops, tell them exactly what your role was in all this and that you were just trying to protect yourself," he said. "What you're doing now will just get you locked up in jail with the key thrown away."

"I can't do jail time," he said.

"You can and will do jail time," he said, "and you'll still have your life at the end of the day."

"Says you," he said. "You have no idea what it's like for guys like me in jail."

"Well, I'm just a little sorry about that, but you should have thought about that before you killed your partner. Anything else was forgivable, but murder? Not so much."

At that, the gunman started to react. "It can't be. I can't go to jail," he cried out, reaching for the gun. And he wrestled with the strength only a full-on panic could bring.

Tucker was forced to use a hard uppercut to clip his chin, knocking him out. He removed the gun from his hand, immediately emptied the chamber, and put the gun into his back pocket. Then he shoved the bullets into the other pocket and pulled out his phone and quickly called the detective.

Addie looked a little more shell-shocked, but she stood firm, keeping her sister in her seat.

"Yeah, you need to come, and you need to come now," he said. "I've got your escaped prisoner. At this point, either he'll try to escape to avoid arrest by taking that bullet that he was hoping for earlier or he'll try shooting his way out of arrest. I have disarmed him at the moment, but things are still volatile."

He pocketed his phone, quickly searched the unconscious gunman to make sure no more weapons were on him, then looked at Addie. "Got anything to tie him up with?"

She raced into the kitchen and came back with zap straps.

He quickly pulled several together and strapped the gunman's hands and feet together. "The detective will be here soon," he said. He turned to look at Bernie, the sister.

"Now what do we do with her?"

"I don't know," Addie said. "What does anybody do with her?"

"There's nothing you can do," Bernie said. "I'll still get that damn dog killed."

"No," he said. "You're not."

She smiled. "Oh, yes," she said. "When you're not expecting it, I'll make sure it's dead."

He stared at her, wondering how he could possibly even think of leaving this woman alive. "It's too bad the gunman didn't shoot you," he said. He could feel Addie staring at him. He looked at her and said, "Sorry, but it's how I feel."

"No," Addie said, "I get it. I felt that way a lot in my life, but she's still somebody I have to deal with."

"Sure but not this way," he said. "She's a threat, keeping a target on our backs."

"Too damn bad," Bernie said. "Because that's what I am, and I'm never going away. I'm like this virus that'll sit here and infect you."

"Well, you'd like to do that to people," he said, "but I'm sure we can charge you with something. After all, you did lie and waste police resources and try to cheat the system, all out of misguided hatred for an animal that did nothing to you." Then he gave her a lethal grin. "I vote for institutionalizing you. You'll have orderlies all around you, kinda like maids but different."

"You're lying," she said, but her voice trembled.

Just then the cops arrived, the sirens so loud it drowned out all voices. The detective walked inside, took one look, and shook his head. "I'm glad he's caught."

The gunman, at this point, was lying on the ground with his eyes open. As the cops stood him up, they had to unclip his hands and feet, and one of the cops came over with handcuffs. Immediately Rural started to fight them. Before they knew it, he suddenly had a gun in his hand. He pointed it at the cop that he'd taken it from. "Now back up slowly."

The cops slowly backed up. Rural looked over at the others. "I'll leave now," he said. "Don't follow."

"That's not possible," the detective said. "You've already killed somebody," he said. "We can't let you go free."

"Too damn bad," he said. He looked over at the sister and sneered. "You should be locking her in jail. She's a true psycho," he said, "but that's probably not happening either. Bitches like her always seem to get away with anything."

And then suddenly he opened fire on Bernie. And he turned the gun just as fast on himself, even before the cops opened fire.

In the shocked silence, Addie smelled the gunpowder.

CHAPTER 14

ADDIE RACED TO her sister's side. But it was too late. A bullet hole was in the center of the woman's head. Addie crouched in front of her sister's body, overwhelmed with pain, shock, grief, all trying to work up through her shoulders. No matter what her sister had been like, she was still her sister. As Addie sat here, the tears rolling down her cheeks, a dog's muzzle slipped up under her arm. She reached down and grabbed Bernie into a great big hug. "Well, you're safe now, sweetheart. At least you're safe."

The dog licked her face gently several times, and she felt some of her grief easing back slightly. This was just such an awful scenario that she had no words for it. She felt ... *relief.* Should she feel that way? Now? Her first voluntary emotion? She had a nagging sense of regret, for what her sister could have been, given different circumstances. Maybe if the family had spoken up earlier, gotten her professional help in terms of long-term hospitalization, they might have avoided this ending? Yet Addie knew, with her nursing background, that treating a patient with multiple mental illnesses made it so much more difficult. The drugs had side effects, didn't work well when combined, masked the symptoms instead of curing them, dulled the patient, even led to suicide when weaning the patient off the drugs. It was a medical conundrum.

She slowly stood, looked at Tucker. He stared at her in worry; she offered a weepy smile. He opened his arms, and she raced into them. She burrowed tight against his chest. "I know she was mean, and she was a bitch," she whispered, "but she didn't deserve this."

"I know, sweetheart. I'm sorry," he said. It took a moment to explain to the detective everything that had gone on.

He stared. "What a hell of a mess," he said.

Addie turned to look at the gunman and the bloody mess around him—Rural was definitely dead too—and Addie immediately turned and buried her face against Tucker's chest. She'd seen enough gunshot wounds in the ER to recognize the devastation. Death spoke a universal language and equalized all people. "Why did it take two more deaths to end this?" she asked nobody in particular. "I can't live here anymore."

"No," Tucker said, "we'll find temporary quarters elsewhere."

"But we gave up the hotel."

"It's okay," he said. "We'll find a new place."

She nodded slowly turned to look at the detective. "I don't know what you would have done with my sister."

"Why?" He looked from her sister's body back to Addie again.

"Because she fabricated the whole thing about the dog biting her to get the dog killed." It took a bit to explain, but she managed to tell him about all the abuse her sister had piled on the poor dog.

He looked at her in shock, shaking his head as he peered at the dead woman, and then turned back to Addie again. Then he said, "I know it's not the right thing to say, but I'm really not unhappy that another bad person is gone right now."

"I know," Addie said. "She had so much potential, but she used it for everything evil," she said. "Still this will be really tough on my parents."

At that, Tucker held her close and said, "They're coming home today, right?"

"Today or tomorrow. I don't know which," she said. "We'll have to contact them to let them know."

"And I'll be there to help you with that," he said firmly.

She smiled and said, "You want to pick that location for a new place for us to live, because I no longer want to be here."

He leaned down, kissed her gently, and said, "I can do that."

She whispered, "Soon?"

"Soon," he said. "I'm staying with you until this is over with," he said. "Not to worry."

She smiled, looked over at the detective. "I know you need statements, and you probably have a mess of questions, so I have to stay here a bit longer. I understand that," she said. "But I just want to go upstairs and lie down for a bit."

"You do that," he said. "We'll touch base later."

"Good," she said, and she, with the dog at her side, walked upstairs and stretched out on her bed. She was so confused. A part of her had hated her sister, despised her. But, when the chips were down, she was still her sister, and her sister was gone, and Addie didn't know if she should feel relief or absolute agony. And it just didn't make any sense. The tears, once started, poured until the well finally emptied. She was dry-eyed but still shaking. In the meantime, she had a whole new future to look after. One that she cared about. One that she wanted to look after and to watch it grow. She looked down to see the dog at her side, worrying. She smiled, patted the bed, and Bernie immediately jumped up beside her, laid down, and Addie hugged Bernie close.

"We'll be together from now on, Bernie. It's okay." The dog waffled gently and leaned in. "I know you were a warrior once too," she said, "but your injuries sidelined you. I know you wanted to attack her, and that would have been bad for you," she said. "It would have given my sister just what she needed to make sure that you didn't get to live anymore," she said, "and that I didn't want to happen."

She heard footsteps coming upstairs and watched as Tucker walked in with a worried look on his face. She smiled and sat up and said, "Bernie was comforting me."

He smiled as he looked down at the two ladies. "My two favorite females in the world."

"Well, outside of your sister," she said gently.

"Absolutely," he said.

"And the police?"

"They'll be here for a while," he said, "but the bodies are gone, and I thought maybe we should go out for a meal or at least move to another hotel to spend the night."

"Do you have one in mind?"

He held up his phone and said, "I've already called one and booked a room, if you are up for it. We can pack an overnight bag and dog food for Bernie. Maybe another bathing suit because I don't think ours ever dried from last night."

She smiled, got up, packed a small bag, looked around at what had once been a beautiful starter home for her for a time, and said, "You know what? Some turning points in your life are when you know that you need to do something different."

"I know," he said, holding out his hand. "This time though you won't be alone."

She smiled, took a step toward him, and, just as she went to join her hand with his, Bernie jumped up between both of them and put her front paws on their joined hands and woofed.

He laughed. "She's right. It's not just the two of us anymore. It's the three of us."

"And," she said, "I'm really good with that."

And, together, as a family, they walked downstairs and into their future.

EPILOGUE

HARLEY BERTRAM WALKED into Badger's office, where he found Geir and Eric as well. Harley slumped into the chair, only to wince and shifted his position.

"How are the injuries these days?" Eric asked.

"Much better than I expected," Harley said. He rotated his wrist. "Some of the surgeries did better than others."

"But you're handling the hammer just fine," Geir noted.

"And the keyboards are getting easier too," he said. "So what's up? Cade said that you were looking for me." He turned and faced Badger.

"Got any dog experience?" Badger asked.

He shrugged. "Outside of the fact that I love them, no."

"No K9 experience in the military?"

"Assisting with the War Dogs, yes," he said, "but I never trained my own. I worked with the training groups," he said. "Man, they were good animals."

"Have you heard about the War Dogs that we've been trying to locate and help?" Badger asked him.

He frowned and shook his head. "I don't know how I missed that," he said, "because, honest to God, it's hard to miss anything in this place."

"True enough," Cade said, walking into the room with a folder. He tossed it on the conference table in front of Badger. "I'm not sure what we'll do with this one," he said.

"I don't know either," Badger said. "I read it early this morning."

"Read what?" Harley asked.

"So this is a male War Dog," Badger explained. "He was adopted and then sold."

"Isn't that against the terms of service of the adoption contract?"

"It absolutely is," he said, "but the adopters didn't seem to care."

"And he was sold to do what?" Harley asked.

"As a security dog," he said.

"Well, that might not be such a bad life."

"Maybe, except it looks like he's in a possible grow op," Cade added.

"Oh no, not drugs," Harley said. "They treat the animals really rough."

"Exactly," Eric said. "So we want to make sure the dog's being well treated and, if he's not, to remove him from the situation."

"But if they bought and paid for him, they might not take too kindly to that suggestion."

"He's the property of the United States government," Badger stated. "Adoptions are done on the understanding that you are looking after the War Dog but do not get to own one."

"Right, and if I get any resistance?"

The three men looked at him.

"Ah," Harley said, "so doesn't matter what kind of resistance there is, I have a job to do."

"Exactly," Badger said. "Unless you got a problem with that."

"Hell no," he said. "I'm much better with fewer rules.

Whereabouts?"

"Montana," Cade said. "He's set up near the Canadian border."

Harley stilled. "I wouldn't have thought the drug-running business or the cannabis business was really good up there."

"Well, that's why we've got a question mark on it," Badger noted. "I'm not exactly sure what you'll find there. But he's supposedly a security dog."

"And legally sold, as far as the new owners know. That could be a bit tough. Any money to help buy the dog back?"

"Some," Geir said. "it just depends on what kind of money we're talking about."

"Right," Harley said, as he stood. "And when do I go?"

"The sooner, the better," Cade stated. "The cops contacted the War Dog department about the dog because another one showed up dead."

"Another War Dog?" Harley gasped.

"No," Badge answered. "another dog and they heard about this one, so they were asking whether it was the same one."

"And the answer, of course, is no."

Badger continued. "I think they were also warning the War Dog department that the particular dog had been abused."

"Great," Harley said under his breath. "Do I get to carry weapons too?"

"What do you want?" Badger asked with interest.

Harley reached out and flexed his hand again and said, "I have a couple of my own."

"I'll get the permits," Badger said, "for travel. I don't want you to go up against a cartel or some such thing without firepower."

"The dog hasn't been there all that long," Cade said. "You might get it on your side and turn it against its owners."

"You know what the answer is for that then," Harley said. "They'll just end up shooting it."

"In that case, why don't you just shoot the gunman," Cade said in a rough voice. "We've seen so many evil assholes in this world," he said. "I get pissed off when somebody like that hurts an animal. Hell, when anybody hurts an animal."

"I hear you." Harley nodded, headed for the door, and said, "I'll check it out and let you know what I find." He stopped and looked back and asked, "Did you guys know that I spent ten years in Montana?"

The men looked at him in surprise.

Harley smiled and said, "I guess not."

"When were you there?" Badger asked.

"I was a foster kid," he said. "I left because I was getting too attached to the family. It seemed like a good idea at the time. I turned eighteen and joined the navy," he said. "And my history since then, you all well know."

"What do you mean, *too attached*?" Badger asked curiously.

He nodded. "The foster family was okay," he said, "but their daughter was dynamite." And, with a wicked grin, he turned and headed out.

Badger called back, "Have you kept in touch with them?"

"No," he said. "So I guess I will now though."

"What's her name?" Geir asked.

"Jasmine," he said. "And she was the sweetest little

thing. Although I couldn't say that to her face." He laughed, stepped across the threshold, then stuck his face back into the doorway. "She is just as likely to shoot me on sight right now."

"Why's that?" Badger frowned at him. "Maybe we shouldn't send you."

"It's all good," he said. "She wanted me to stay, and I didn't dare."

"Why?" Cade asked.

"Her family. I wasn't good enough," he said. "Believe me. I won't be good enough now either."

"Maybe they've changed," Eric said with a one-arm shrug.

"Maybe," he said, "but I haven't."

This concludes Book 13 of The K9 Files: Tucker.

Read about Harley: The K9 Files, Book 14

THE K9 FILES: HARLEY (BOOK #14)

Welcome to the all new K9 Files series reconnecting readers with the unforgettable men from SEALs of Steel in a new series of action packed, page turning romantic suspense that fans have come to expect from USA TODAY Bestselling author Dale Mayer. Pssst... you'll meet other favorite characters from SEALs of Honor and Heroes for Hire too!

Returning to the town he was raised in was hard, except that Harley can once more see the only golden light of those days. He'd walked away from her because she'd been too young, and he would never be good enough. Harley was back to check on the War Dog Bowser, but Harley can't help but feel like he never really left. But when Harley snags the War Dog from one of Bowser's handlers, Harley knows he has to put a stop to this guy forever.

Over all these years Jasmine awaits Harley's return, but he won't be happy with the changes she's gone through. When he shows up out of the blue, she knows only complete honesty will be good enough. But it was rough and meant opening up memories of a horrible time in her life.

Harley's arrival prompts a hidden truth that someone will do anything to stop from coming out. And Harley will do everything he can to get justice for her ...

Find Book 14 here!
To find out more visit Dale Mayer's website.
https://geni.us/DMHarleyUniversal

Author's Note

Thank you for reading Tucker: The K9 Files, Book 13! If you enjoyed the book, please take a moment and leave a short review.

Dear reader,

I love to hear from readers, and you can contact me at my website: www.dalemayer.com or at my Facebook author page. To be informed of new releases and special offers, sign up for my newsletter or follow me on BookBub. And if you are interested in joining Dale Mayer's Reader Group, here is the Facebook sign up page.
http://geni.us/DaleMayerFBGroup

Cheers,
Dale Mayer

About the Author

Dale Mayer is a *USA Today* best-selling author, best known for her SEALs military romances, her Psychic Visions series, and her Lovely Lethal Garden cozy series. Her contemporary romances are raw and full of passion and emotion (Broken But ... Mending, Hathaway House series). Her thrillers will keep you guessing (Kate Morgan, By Death series), and her romantic comedies will keep you giggling (*It's a Dog's Life*, a stand-alone novella; and the Broken Protocols series, starring Charming Marvin, the cat).

Dale honors the stories that come to her—and some of them are crazy, break all the rules and cross multiple genres!

To go with her fiction, she also writes nonfiction in many different fields, with books available on résumé writing, companion gardening, and the US mortgage system. All her books are available in print and ebook format.

Connect with Dale Mayer Online

Dale's Website – www.dalemayer.com
Twitter – @DaleMayer
Facebook Page – geni.us/DaleMayerFBFanPage
Facebook Group – geni.us/DaleMayerFBGroup
BookBub – geni.us/DaleMayerBookbub
Instagram – geni.us/DaleMayerInstagram
Goodreads – geni.us/DaleMayerGoodreads
Newsletter – geni.us/DaleNews

Also by Dale Mayer

Published Adult Books:

Hathaway House
Aaron, Book 1
Brock, Book 2
Cole, Book 3
Denton, Book 4
Elliot, Book 5
Finn, Book 6
Gregory, Book 7
Heath, Book 8
Iain, Book 9
Jaden, Book 10
Keith, Book 11
Lance, Book 12
Melissa, Book 13
Nash, Book 14
Owen, Book 15
Hathaway House, Books 1–3
Hathaway House, Books 4–6
Hathaway House, Books 7–9

The K9 Files
Ethan, Book 1
Pierce, Book 2
Zane, Book 3

Lovely Lethal Gardens

Psychic Vision Series
Tuesday's Child
Hide 'n Go Seek
Maddy's Floor
Garden of Sorrow
Knock Knock…
Rare Find
Eyes to the Soul
Now You See Her
Shattered
Into the Abyss
Seeds of Malice
Eye of the Falcon
Itsy-Bitsy Spider
Unmasked
Deep Beneath
From the Ashes
Stroke of Death
Ice Maiden
Psychic Visions Books 1–3
Psychic Visions Books 4–6
Psychic Visions Books 7–9

By Death Series
Touched by Death
Haunted by Death
Chilled by Death
By Death Books 1–3

Broken Protocols – Romantic Comedy Series
Cat's Meow
Cat's Pajamas

Cat's Cradle
Cat's Claus
Broken Protocols 1-4

Broken and... Mending
Skin
Scars
Scales (of Justice)
Broken but... Mending 1-3

Glory
Genesis
Tori
Celeste
Glory Trilogy

Biker Blues
Morgan: Biker Blues, Volume 1
Cash: Biker Blues, Volume 2

SEALs of Honor
Mason: SEALs of Honor, Book 1
Hawk: SEALs of Honor, Book 2
Dane: SEALs of Honor, Book 3
Swede: SEALs of Honor, Book 4
Shadow: SEALs of Honor, Book 5
Cooper: SEALs of Honor, Book 6
Markus: SEALs of Honor, Book 7
Evan: SEALs of Honor, Book 8
Mason's Wish: SEALs of Honor, Book 9
Chase: SEALs of Honor, Book 10
Brett: SEALs of Honor, Book 11
Devlin: SEALs of Honor, Book 12

Easton: SEALs of Honor, Book 13
Ryder: SEALs of Honor, Book 14
Macklin: SEALs of Honor, Book 15
Corey: SEALs of Honor, Book 16
Warrick: SEALs of Honor, Book 17
Tanner: SEALs of Honor, Book 18
Jackson: SEALs of Honor, Book 19
Kanen: SEALs of Honor, Book 20
Nelson: SEALs of Honor, Book 21
Taylor: SEALs of Honor, Book 22
Colton: SEALs of Honor, Book 23
Troy: SEALs of Honor, Book 24
Axel: SEALs of Honor, Book 25
Baylor: SEALs of Honor, Book 26
SEALs of Honor, Books 1–3
SEALs of Honor, Books 4–6
SEALs of Honor, Books 7–10
SEALs of Honor, Books 11–13
SEALs of Honor, Books 14–16
SEALs of Honor, Books 17–19
SEALs of Honor, Books 20–22
SEALs of Honor, Books 23–25

Heroes for Hire

Levi's Legend: Heroes for Hire, Book 1
Stone's Surrender: Heroes for Hire, Book 2
Merk's Mistake: Heroes for Hire, Book 3
Rhodes's Reward: Heroes for Hire, Book 4
Flynn's Firecracker: Heroes for Hire, Book 5
Logan's Light: Heroes for Hire, Book 6
Harrison's Heart: Heroes for Hire, Book 7
Saul's Sweetheart: Heroes for Hire, Book 8

SEALs of Steel

SEALs of Steel, Books 1–4
SEALs of Steel, Books 5–8
SEALs of Steel, Books 1–8

The Mavericks
Kerrick, Book 1
Griffin, Book 2
Jax, Book 3
Beau, Book 4
Asher, Book 5
Ryker, Book 6
Miles, Book 7
Nico, Book 8
Keane, Book 9
Lennox, Book 10
Gavin, Book 11
Shane, Book 12

Bullard's Battle Series
Ryland's Reach, Book 1
Cain's Cross, Book 2
Eton's Escape, Book 3
Garret's Gambit, Book 4
Kano's Keep, Book 5
Fallon's Flaw, Book 6
Quinn's Quest, Book 7
Bullard's Beauty, Book 8

Collections
Dare to Be You...
Dare to Love...
Dare to be Strong...

RomanceX3

Standalone Novellas
It's a Dog's Life
Riana's Revenge
Second Chances

Published Young Adult Books:

Family Blood Ties Series
Vampire in Denial
Vampire in Distress
Vampire in Design
Vampire in Deceit
Vampire in Defiance
Vampire in Conflict
Vampire in Chaos
Vampire in Crisis
Vampire in Control
Vampire in Charge
Family Blood Ties Set 1–3
Family Blood Ties Set 1–5
Family Blood Ties Set 4–6
Family Blood Ties Set 7–9
Sian's Solution, A Family Blood Ties Series Prequel
    Novelette

Design series
Dangerous Designs
Deadly Designs
Darkest Designs
Design Series Trilogy

Standalone

In Cassie's Corner
Gem Stone (a Gemma Stone Mystery)
Time Thieves

Published Non-Fiction Books:

Career Essentials

Career Essentials: The Résumé
Career Essentials: The Cover Letter
Career Essentials: The Interview
Career Essentials: 3 in 1

Made in the USA
Monee, IL
05 January 2025

75794028R00128